MILNE'S HIGH SCHOOL.

1. This book is the property of Milne's High School, Fochabers, Moray.
2. The pupil to whom it is issued is responsible for its safe keeping and good condition.
3. Any damage to the book or loss should be reported without delay to the Class Teacher or Rector.
4. A pupil who loses or misuses a class text-book will be required to replace it or refund its value.
5. If the pupil or another member of the household is suffering from a contagious disease, the Rector should be informed.
6. This book must be covered by the pupil to whom it is issued.
7. It will be appreciated if any person finding this book will return it to the School.

Date of Issue	Name of Pupil	Class
25/8/66	Robert Jarrold	TIP
6"1"66	Jackie Cowie	II
22.8.67	Linda McIntosh	TIP

J. M. & S., K.

The KINGS TREASURIES
OF LITERATURE

GENERAL EDITOR
Sir A·T· QUILLER COUCH

LONDON : J·M·DENT & SONS LTD.

THE KING OF THE GOLDEN RIVER
OR THE
BLACK BROTHERS

A LEGEND OF STYRIA

ADVERTISEMENT
TO THE FIRST EDITION

THE Publishers think it due to the Author of this Fairy Tale, to state the circumstances under which it appears.

The King of the Golden River was written in 1841, at the request of a very young lady, and solely for her amusement, without any idea of publication. It has since remained in the possession of a friend, to whose suggestion, and the passive assent of the Author, the Publishers are indebted for the opportunity of printing it.

The Illustrations, by Mr. Richard Doyle, will, it is hoped, be found to embody the Author's ideas with characteristic spirit.

PUBLISHERS' NOTE
TO THE PRESENT EDITION

THE pictures have been used so often that, like many other good things, they are worn in the service of the public. They are, however, part of the book, and were produced by those princes of engraving the Brothers Dalziel, who worked not only with Doyle but also with Millais, Holman Hunt, Arthur Hughes and other great illustrators of the 'sixties. Under the circumstances the publishers of the present edition felt that readers would prefer them with all their technical imperfections to new illustrations by another hand.

CONTENTS

THE
KING OF THE GOLDEN RIVER

BY

JOHN RUSKIN

THE KING
OF THE GOLDEN RIVER

CHAPTER I

HOW THE AGRICULTURAL SYSTEM OF THE BLACK
BROTHERS WAS INTERFERED WITH BY SOUTH
WEST WIND, ESQUIRE

A secluded and mountainous
part of Stiria, there was, in old
time, a valley of the most surpris-
ing and luxuriant fertility. It was
surrounded, on all sides, by steep
and rocky mountains, rising into
peaks, which were always covered with snow, and from
which a number of torrents descended in constant
cataracts. One of these fell westward, over the face
of a crag so high, that, when the sun had set to everything else, and all below was darkness, his beams
still shone full upon this waterfall, so that it looked

like a shower of gold. It was, therefore, called by the people of the neighbourhood, the Golden River.

It was strange that none of these streams fell into the valley itself. They all descended on the other side of the mountains, and wound away through broad plains and by populous cities. But the clouds were drawn so constantly to the snowy hills, and rested so softly in the circular hollow, that in time of drought and heat, when all the country round was burnt up, there was still rain in the little valley; and its crops were so heavy, and its hay so high, and its apples so red, and its grapes so blue, and its wine so rich, and its honey so sweet, that it was a marvel to every one who beheld it, and was commonly called the Treasure Valley.

The whole of this little valley belonged to three brothers, called Schwartz, Hans, and Gluck. Schwartz and Hans, the two elder brothers, were very ugly men, with overhanging eyebrows and small dull eyes, which were always half-shut, so that you couldn't see into *them*, and always fancied they saw very far into *you*.

They lived by farming the Treasure Valley, and very good farmers they were. They killed everything that did not pay for its eating. They shot the black-birds, because they pecked the fruit; and killed the hedgehogs, lest they should suck the cows; they poisoned the crickets for eating the crumbs in the kitchen, and smothered the cicadas, which used to sing all summer in the lime trees. They worked their servants without any wages, till they would not work any more, and then quarrelled with them, and turned them out of doors without paying them.

It would have been very odd, if with such a farm, and such a system of farming, they hadn't got very rich; and very rich they *did* get. They generally contrived to keep their corn by them till it was very dear, and then sell it for twice its value; they had heaps of gold lying about on their floors, yet it was never known that they had given so much as a penny or a crust to charity; they never went to mass; grumbled perpetually at paying tithes; and were, in a word, of so cruel and grinding a temper, as to receive from all those with whom they had any dealings, the nickname of the "Black Brothers."

The youngest brother, Gluck, was as completely opposed, in both appearance and character, to his seniors as could possibly be imagined or desired. He was not above twelve years old, fair, blue-eyed, and kind in temper to every living thing. He did not, of course, agree particularly well with his brothers, or rather, they did not agree with *him*. He was usually appointed to the honourable office of turnspit, when there was anything to roast, which was not often; for, to do the brothers justice, they were hardly less sparing upon themselves than upon other people. At other times he used to clean the shoes, floors, and sometimes the plates, occasionally getting what was left on them, by way of encouragement, and a wholesome quantity of dry blows, by way of education.

Things went on in this manner for a long time. At last came a very wet summer, and everything went wrong in the country round. The hay had hardly been got in, when the haystacks were floated bodily down to the sea by an inundation; the vines were cut to pieces with the hail; the corn was all killed by a black blight; only in the Treasure Valley, as usual, all was safe. As it had rain when there was rain nowhere else, so it had sun when there was sun nowhere else. Everybody came to buy corn at the farm, and went away pouring maledictions on the Black Brothers. They asked what they liked, and got it, except from the poor people, who could only beg, and several of whom were starved at their very door, without the slightest regard or notice.

It was drawing towards winter, and very cold weather, when one day the two elder brothers had gone out, with their usual warning to little Gluck, who was left to mind the roast, that he was to let nobody in, and give nothing out. Gluck sat down quite close to the fire, for it was raining very hard, and the kitchen walls were by no means dry or comfortable looking. He turned and turned, and the roast got nice and brown. "What a pity," thought Gluck, "my brothers never ask anybody to dinner. I'm sure, when they've got such a nice piece of mutton as this, and nobody else has got so much as a piece of dry bread, it would do their hearts good to have somebody to eat it with them."

Just as he spoke, there came a double knock at the

house door, yet heavy and dull, as though the knocker had been tied up—more like a puff than a knock. "It must be the wind," said Gluck; "nobody else would venture to knock double knocks at our door." No, it wasn't the wind: there it came again very hard, and what was particularly astounding, the knocker seemed to be in a hurry, and not to be in the least afraid of the consequences.

Gluck went to the window, opened it, and put his head out to see who it was. It was the most extra-ordinary-looking little gentleman he had ever seen in his life. He had a very long nose, slightly brass-coloured, and expanding towards its termination into a development not unlike the lower extremity of a key bugle. His cheeks were very round, and very red, and might have warranted a supposition that he had been blowing a refractory fire for the last eight-and-forty hours. His eyes twinkled merrily through long silky eyelashes, his moustaches curled twice round like a corkscrew on each side of his mouth, and his hair, of a curious mixed pepper-and-salt colour, descended far over his shoulders.

He was about four feet six in height, and wore a conical pointed cap of nearly the same altitude, decorated with a black feather some three feet long. His doublet was prolonged behind into something resembling a violent exaggeration of what is now termed a "swallow tail," but was much obscured by the swelling folds of an enormous black, glossy-looking cloak, which must have been very much too

long in calm weather, as the wind, whistling round
the old house, carried it clear out from the wearer's
shoulders to about four times his own length.

Gluck was so perfectly paralysed by the singular
appearance of his visitor, that he remained fixed
without uttering a word, until the old gentleman,
having performed another, and a more energetic
concerto on the knocker, turned round to look after
his fly-away cloak. In so doing he caught sight of
Gluck's little yellow head jammed in the window,
with its mouth and eyes very wide open indeed.

"Hollo!" said the little gentleman, "that's not
the way to answer the door: I'm wet, let me in."

To do the little gentleman justice, he *was* wet.
His feather hung down between his legs like a beaten
puppy's tail, dripping like an umbrella; and from the
ends of his moustaches the water was running into
his waistcoat pockets, and out again like a mill-stream.

"I beg pardon, sir," said Gluck, "I'm very sorry,
but I really can't."

"Can't what?" said the old gentleman.

"I can't let you in, sir,—I can't indeed; my
brothers would beat me to death, sir, if I thought
of such a thing. What do you want, sir?"

"Want?" said the old gentleman petulantly. "I
want fire, and shelter; and there's your great fire
there blazing, crackling, and dancing on the walls,
with nobody to feel it. Let me in, I say; I only want
to warm myself."

Gluck had had his head, by this time, so long out

of the window, that he began to feel it was really
unpleasantly cold, and when he turned, and saw the
beautiful fire rustling and roaring, and throwing
long bright tongues up the chimney, as if it were
licking its chops at the savoury smell of the leg of
mutton, his heart melted within him that it should
be burning away for nothing. "He does look *very*
wet," said little Gluck; "I'll just let him in for a
quarter of an hour." Round he went to the door
and opened it; and as the little gentleman walked
in, there came a gust of wind through the house that
made the old chimneys totter.

"That's a good boy," said the little gentleman.
"Never mind your brothers. I'll talk to them."

"Pray, sir, don't do any such thing," said Gluck.
"I can't let you stay till they come; they'd be the
death of me."

"Dear me," said the old gentleman, "I'm very
sorry to hear that. How long may I stay?"

"Only till the mutton's done, sir," replied Gluck,
"and it's very brown."

Then the old gentleman walked into the kitchen,
and sat himself down on the hob, with the top of
his cap accommodated up the chimney, for it was a
great deal too high for the roof.

"You'll soon dry there, sir," said Gluck, and sat
down again to turn the mutton. But the old gentleman did *not* dry there, but went on drip, drip, dripping
among the cinders, and the fire fizzed, and sputtered,
and began to look very black, and uncomfortable;

never was such a cloak; every fold in it ran like a gutter.

"I beg pardon, sir," said Gluck at length, after watching the water spreading in long, quicksilver-like streams over the floor for a quarter of an hour; "mayn't I take your cloak?"

"No, thank you," said the old gentleman.

"Your cap, sir?"

"I am all right, thank you," said the old gentleman rather gruffly.

"But,—sir,—I'm very sorry," said Gluck, hesitatingly; "but—really, sir,—you're—putting the fire out."

"It'll take longer to do the mutton then," replied his visitor drily.

Gluck was very much puzzled by the behaviour

of his guest; it was such a strange mixture of coolness and humility. He turned away at the string meditatively for another five minutes.

"That mutton looks very nice," said the old gentleman at length. "Can't you give me a little bit?"

"Impossible, sir," said Gluck.

"I'm very hungry," continued the old gentleman. "I've had nothing to eat yesterday, nor to-day. They surely couldn't miss a bit from the knuckle!"

He spoke in so very melancholy a tone, that it quite melted Gluck's heart. "They promised me one slice to-day, sir," said he. "I can give you that, but not a bit more."

"That's a good boy," said the old gentleman again.

Then Gluck warmed a plate, and sharpened a knife. "I don't care if I do get beaten for it," thought he. Just as he had cut a large slice out of the mutton, there came a tremendous rap at the door. The old gentleman jumped off the hob, as if it had suddenly become inconveniently warm. Gluck fitted the slice into the mutton again, with desperate efforts at exactitude, and ran to open the door.

"What did you keep us waiting in the rain for?" said Schwartz, as he walked in, throwing his umbrella in Gluck's face. "Ay! what for, indeed, you little vagabond?" said Hans, administering an educational box on the ear, as he followed his brother into the kitchen.

"Bless my soul!" said Schwartz when he opened the door.

"Amen," said the little gentleman, who had taken his cap off, and was standing in the middle of the kitchen, bowing with the utmost possible velocity.

"Who's that?" said Schwartz, catching up a rolling-pin, and turning to Gluck with a fierce frown.

"I don't know, indeed, brother," said Gluck in great terror.

"How did he get in?" roared Schwartz.

"My dear brother," said Gluck, deprecatingly, "he was so *very* wet!"

The rolling-pin was descending on Gluck's head; but, at the instant, the old gentleman interposed his conical cap, on which it crashed with a shock that shook the water out of it all over the room. What was very odd, the rolling-pin no sooner touched the cap than it flew out of Schwartz's hand, spinning like a straw in a high wind, and fell into the corner at the farther end of the room.

"Who are you, sir?" demanded Schwartz, turning upon him.

"What's your business?" snarled Hans.

"I'm a poor old man, sir," the little gentleman began very modestly, "and I saw your fire through the window, and begged shelter for a quarter of an hour."

"Have the goodness to walk out again, then," said Schwartz. "We've quite enough water in our kitchen, without making it a drying-house."

"It is a cold day to turn an old man out in, sir; look at my grey hairs." They hung down to his shoulders, as I told you before.

"Ay!" said Hans, "there are enough of them to keep you warm. Walk!"

"I'm very, very hungry, sir; couldn't you spare me a bit of bread before I go?"

"Bread, indeed!" said Schwartz; "do you suppose we've nothing to do with our bread but to give it to such red-nosed fellows as you?"

"Why don't you sell your feather?" said Hans, sneeringly. "Out with you."

"A little bit," said the old gentleman.

"Be off!" said Schwartz.

"Pray, gentlemen."

"Off, and be hanged!" cried Hans, seizing him by the collar. But he had no sooner touched the old gentleman's collar than away he went after the rolling-pin, spinning round and round, till he fell into the corner on the top of it. Then Schwartz was very angry, and ran at the old gentleman to turn him out; but he also had hardly touched him, when away he went after Hans and the rolling-pin, and hit his head against the wall as he tumbled into the corner. And so there they lay, all three.

Then the old gentleman spun himself round with velocity in the opposite direction; continued to spin until his long cloak was all wound neatly about him; clapped his cap on his head, very much on one side (for it could not stand upright without going through the ceiling), gave an additional twist to his corkscrew moustaches, and replied with perfect coolness: "Gentlemen, I wish you a very good morning. At twelve o'clock to-night I'll call again; after such a refusal of hospitality as I have just experienced, you will not be surprised if that visit is the last I ever pay you."

"If ever I catch you here again," muttered Schwartz, coming half-frightened out of the corner —but, before he could finish his sentence, the old gentleman had shut the house door behind him with a great bang: and there drove past the window, at the same instant, a wreath of ragged cloud, that whirled and rolled away down the valley in all manner of shapes; turning over and over in the air; and melting away at last in a gush of rain.

"A very pretty business, indeed, Mr. Gluck!" said Schwartz. "Dish the mutton, sir. If ever I catch you at such a trick again—bless me, why the mutton's been cut!"

"You promised me one slice, brother, you know," said Gluck.

"Oh! and you were cutting it hot, I suppose, and going to catch all the gravy. It'll be long before I promise you such a thing again. Leave the room, sir; and have the kindness to wait in the coal-cellar till I call you."

Gluck left the room, melancholy enough. The brothers ate as much mutton as they could, locked the rest in the cupboard, and proceeded to get very drunk after dinner.

Such a night as it was! Howling wind, and rushing rain, without intermission. The brothers had just sense enough left to put up all the shutters, and double bar the door, before they went to bed. They usually slept in the same room. As the clock struck twelve, they were both awakened by a tremendous crash. Their door burst open with a violence that shook the house from top to bottom.

"What's that?" cried Schwartz, starting up in his bed.

"Only I," said the little gentleman.

The two brothers sat up on their bolster, and stared into the darkness. The room was full of water, and by a misty moonbeam, which found its way through a hole in the shutter, they could see in the midst of it an enormous foam globe, spinning round, and bobbing up and down like a cork, on which, as on a most

luxurious cushion, reclined the little old gentleman,
cap and all. There was plenty of room for it now, for
the roof was off.

"Sorry to incommode you," said their visitor,
ironically. "I'm afraid your beds are dampish;
perhaps you had better go to your brother's room:
I've left the ceiling on, there."

They required no second admonition, but rushed

into Gluck's room, wet through, and in an agony
of terror.

"You'll find my card on the kitchen table," the
old gentleman called after them. "Remember, the
last visit."

"Pray Heaven it may!" said Schwartz, shuddering. And the foam globe disappeared.

Dawn came at last, and the two brothers looked
out of Gluck's little window in the morning. The
Treasure Valley was one mass of ruin and desolation.

The inundation had swept away trees, crops, and cattle, and left in their stead a waste of red sand and grey mud. The two brothers crept shivering and horror-struck into the kitchen. The water had gutted the whole first floor; corn, money, almost every movable thing had been swept away, and there was left only a small white card on the kitchen table. On it, in large, breezy, long-legged letters, were engraved the words:

CHAPTER II

SOUTH WEST WIND, ESQUIRE, was as good as his word. After the momentous visit above related, he entered the Treasure Valley no more; and, what was worse, he had so much influence with his relations, the West Winds in general, and used it so effectually, that they all adopted a similar line of conduct. So no rain fell in the valley from one year's end to another. Though everything remained green and flourishing in the plains below, the inheritance of the Three Brothers was a desert. What had once been the richest soil in the kingdom, became a shifting heap of red sand; and the brothers, unable longer to contend with the adverse skies, abandoned their valueless patrimony in despair, to seek some means of gaining a livelihood among the cities and people of the plains. All their money was gone, and they had nothing left but some curious old-fashioned pieces of gold plate, the last remnants of their ill-gotten wealth.

"Suppose we turn goldsmiths?" said Schwartz to Hans, as they entered the large city. "It is a good knave's trade; we can put a great deal of copper into the gold, without any one's finding it out."

The thought was agreed to be a very good one; they hired a furnace, and turned goldsmiths. But two slight circumstances affected their trade: the first, that people did not approve of the coppered gold; the second, that the two elder brothers, whenever

they had sold anything, used to leave little Gluck
to mind the furnace, and go and drink out the money
in the ale-house next door. So they melted all their
gold, without making money enough to buy more,
and were at last reduced to one large drinking-mug,
which an uncle of his had given to little Gluck, and
which he was very fond of, and would not have parted
with for the world; though he never drank anything
out of it but milk and water. The mug was a very
odd mug to look at. The handle was formed of two
wreaths of flowing golden hair, so finely spun that
it looked more like silk than metal, and these wreaths
descended into and mixed with a beard and whiskers,
of the same exquisite workmanship, which surrounded
and decorated a very fierce little face, of the reddest
gold imaginable, right in the front of the mug, with
a pair of eyes in it which seemed to command its
whole circumference. It was impossible to drink out
of the mug without being subjected to an intense
gaze out of the side of these eyes; and Schwartz
positively averred, that once, after emptying it, full
of Rhenish, seventeen times, he had seen them wink!
When it came to the mug's turn to be made into
spoons, it half-broke poor little Gluck's heart; but the
brothers only laughed at him, tossed the mug into
the melting-pot, and staggered out to the ale-house;
leaving him, as usual, to pour the gold into bars,
when it was all ready.

When they were gone, Gluck took a farewell look
at his old friend in the melting-pot. The flowing hair

was all gone; nothing remained but the red nose, and the sparkling eyes, which looked more malicious than ever. "And no wonder," thought Gluck, "after being treated in that way." He sauntered disconsolately to the window, and sat him-self down to catch the fresh evening air, and escape the hot breath of the furnace. Now this window com-manded a direct view of the range of mountains, which, as I told you before, over-hung the Treasure Valley, and more especially of the peak from which fell the

Golden River. It was just at the close of the day, and, when Gluck sat down at the window, he saw the rocks of the mountain tops, all crimson and purple with the sunset; and there were bright tongues of fiery cloud burning and quivering about them; and the river, brighter than all, fell, in a waving column of pure gold, from precipice to precipice, with the double arch of a broad purple rainbow stretched across it, flushing and fading alternately in the wreaths of spray.

"Ah!" said Gluck aloud, after he had looked at it for a little while, "if that river were really all gold, what a nice thing it would be."

"No, it wouldn't, Gluck," said a clear metallic voice close at his ear.

"Bless me, what's that?" exclaimed Gluck, jumping up. There was nobody there. He looked round the room, and under the table, and a great many times behind him, but there was certainly nobody there, and he sat down again at the window. This time he didn't speak, but he couldn't help thinking again that it would be very convenient if the river were really all gold.

"Not at all, my boy," said the same voice, louder than before.

"Bless me!" said Gluck again, "what *is* that?" He looked again into all the corners and cupboards, and then began turning round and round, as fast as he could, in the middle of the room, thinking there was somebody behind him, when the same voice struck again on his ear. It was singing now very merrily "Lala-lira-la"; no words, only a soft running effervescent melody, something like that of a kettle on the boil. Gluck looked out of the window. No, it was certainly in the house. Up stairs and down stairs. No, it was certainly in that very room, coming in quicker time, and clearer notes, every moment. "Lala-lira-la." All at once it struck Gluck that it sounded louder near the furnace. He ran to the opening, and looked in: yes, he was right, it seemed to be coming, not only out of the furnace, but out of the pot. He uncovered it, and ran back in a great fright, for the pot was certainly singing! He stood in the farthest corner of the room, with his hands up, and his mouth open, for a minute or two, when the singing stopped, and the voice became clear and pronunciative.

"Hollo!" said the voice.

Gluck made no answer.

"Hollo! Gluck, my boy," said the pot again.

Gluck summoned all his energies, walked straight up to the crucible, drew it out of the furnace, and looked in. The gold was all melted, and its surface as smooth and polished as a river; but instead of reflecting little Gluck's head, as he looked in, he saw meeting his glance, from beneath the gold, the red nose and sharp eyes of his old friend of the mug, a thousand times redder and sharper than ever he had seen them in his life.

"Come, Gluck, my boy," said the voice out of the pot again, "I'm all right; pour me out."

But Gluck was too much astonished to do anything of the kind.

"Pour me out, I say," said the voice rather gruffly.

Still Gluck couldn't move.

"*Will* you pour me out?" said the voice passionately; "I'm too hot."

By a violent effort, Gluck recovered the use of his limbs, took hold of the crucible, and sloped it, so as to pour out the gold. But instead of a liquid stream, there came out, first, a pair of pretty little yellow legs, then some coat-tails, then a pair of arms stuck a-kimbo, and, finally, the well-known head of his friend the mug; all which articles, uniting as they rolled out, stood up energetically on the floor, in the shape of a little golden dwarf, about a foot and a half high.

"That's right!" said the dwarf, stretching out first his legs, and then his arms, and then shaking his

head up and down, and as far round as it would go, for five minutes, without stopping; apparently with the view of ascertaining if he were quite correctly put together, while Gluck stood contemplating him in speechless amazement. He was dressed in a slashed

doublet of spun gold, so fine in its texture that the
prismatic colours gleamed over it, as if on a surface
of mother-of-pearl; and, over this brilliant doublet,
his hair and beard fell full half way to the ground,
in waving curls, so exquisitely delicate, that Gluck
could hardly tell where they ended; they seemed to
melt into air. The features of the face, however, were
by no means finished with the same delicacy; they
were rather coarse, slightly inclining to coppery in
complexion, and indicative, in expression, of a very
pertinacious and intractable disposition in their
small proprietor. When the dwarf had finished his
self-examination, he turned his small sharp eyes full
on Gluck, and stared at him deliberately for a minute
or two. "No it wouldn't, Gluck, my boy," said the
little man.

This was certainly rather an abrupt and un-
connected mode of commencing conversation. It
might indeed be supposed to refer to the course of
Gluck's thoughts, which had first produced the dwarf's
observations out of the pot; but whatever it referred
to, Gluck had no inclination to dispute the dictum.

"Wouldn't it, sir?" said Gluck, very mildly and
submissively indeed.

"No," said the dwarf, conclusively. "No it
wouldn't." And with that, the dwarf pulled his cap
hard over his brows, and took two turns, of three
feet long, up and down the room, lifting his legs up
very high, and setting them down very hard. This
pause gave time for Gluck to collect his thoughts a

little; and, seeing no great reason to view his diminutive visitor with dread, and feeling his curiosity overcome his amazement, he ventured on a question of peculiar delicacy.

"Pray, sir," said Gluck, rather hesitatingly, "were you my mug?"

On which the little man turned sharp round, walked straight up to Gluck, and drew himself up to his full height. "I," said the little man, "am the King of the Golden River." Whereupon he turned about again, and took two more turns, some six feet long, in order to allow time for the consternation which this announcement produced in his auditor to evaporate. After which, he again walked up to Gluck and stood still, as if expecting some comment on his communication.

Gluck determined to say something at all events. "I hope your majesty is very well," said Gluck.

"Listen!" said the little man, deigning no reply to this polite inquiry. "I am the King of what you mortals call the Golden River. The shape you saw me in was owing to the malice of a stronger king, from whose enchantments you have this instant freed me. What I have seen of you, and your conduct to your wicked brothers, renders me willing to serve you; therefore attend to what I tell you. Whoever shall climb to the top of that mountain from which you see the Golden River issue, and shall cast into the stream at its source three drops of holy water, for him, and for him only, the river shall turn to gold.

But no one failing in his first, can succeed in a second attempt; and if any one shall cast unholy water into the river, it will overwhelm him, and he will become a black stone." So saying, the King of the Golden River turned away, and deliberately walked into the centre of the hottest flame of the furnace. His figure became red, white, transparent, dazzling—a blaze of intense light—rose, trembled, and disappeared. The King of the Golden River had evaporated.

"Oh!" cried poor Gluck, running to look up the chimney after him. "Oh, dear, dear, dear me! My mug! my mug! my mug!"

CHAPTER III

THE King of the Golden River had hardly made the extraordinary exit related in the last chapter, before Hans and Schwartz came roaring into the house, very savagely drunk. The discovery of the total loss of their last piece of plate had the effect of sobering them just enough to enable them to stand over Gluck, beating him very steadily for a quarter of an hour; at the expiration of which period they dropped into a couple of chairs, and requested to know what he had got to say for himself. Gluck told them his story, of which of course they did not believe a word. They beat him again, till their arms were tired, and staggered to bed. In the morning, however, the steadiness with which he adhered to his story obtained him some degree of credence; the immediate consequence of which was, that the two brothers, after wrangling a long time on the knotty question, which of them should try his fortune first, drew their swords and began fighting. The noise of the fray alarmed the neighbours, who, finding they could not pacify the combatants, sent for the constable.

Hans, on hearing this, contrived to escape, and hid himself; but Schwartz was taken before the magis-

trate, fined for breaking the peace, and, having drunk out his last penny the evening before, was thrown into prison till he should pay.

When Hans heard this, he was much delighted, and determined to set out immediately for the Golden River. How to get the holy water, was the question. He went to the priest, but the priest could not give any holy water to so abandoned a character. So Hans went to vespers in the evening for the first time in his life, and, under pretence of crossing himself, stole a cupful, and returned home in triumph.

Next morning he got up before the sun rose, put the holy water into a strong flask, and two bottles of wine and some meat in a basket, slung them over his back, took his alpine staff in his hand, and set off for the mountains.

On his way out of the town he had to pass the prison, and as he looked in at the windows, whom should he

see but Schwartz himself peeping out of the bars, and looking very disconsolate.

"Good morning, brother," said Hans; "have you any message for the King of the Golden River?"

Schwartz gnashed his teeth with rage, and shook the bars with all his strength; but Hans only laughed at him, and, advising him to make himself comfortable till he came back again, shouldered his basket, shook the bottle of holy water in Schwartz's face till it frothed again, and marched off in the highest spirits in the world.

It was, indeed, a morning that might have made

any one happy, even with no Golden River to seek for. Level lines of dewy mist lay stretched along the valley, out of which rose the massy mountains— their lower cliffs in pale grey shadow, hardly distinguishable from the floating vapour, but gradually ascending till they caught the sunlight, which ran in sharp touches of ruddy colour along the angular crags, and pierced, in long level rays, through their fringes of spear-like pine. Far above, shot up red splintered masses of castellated rock, jagged and shivered into myriads of fantastic forms, with here and there a streak of sunlit snow, traced down their chasms like a line of forked lightning; and, far beyond, and far above all these, fainter than the morning cloud, but purer and changeless, slept, in the blue sky, the utmost peaks of the eternal snow.

The Golden River, which sprang from one of the lower and snowless elevations, was now nearly in shadow; all but the uppermost jets of spray, which rose like slow smoke above the undulating line of the cataract, and floated away in feeble wreaths upon the morning wind.

On this object, and on this alone, Hans' eyes and thoughts were fixed; forgetting the distance he had to traverse, he set off at an imprudent rate of walking, which greatly exhausted him before he had scaled the first range of the green and low hills. He was, moreover, surprised, on surmounting them, to find that a large glacier, of whose existence, notwithstanding his previous knowledge of the mountains,

he had been absolutely ignorant, lay between him
and the source of the Golden River. He entered on
it with the boldness of a practised mountaineer;
yet he thought he had never traversed so strange
or so dangerous a glacier in his life.

The ice was excessively slippery, and out of all
its chasms came wild sounds of gushing water; not
monotonous or low, but changeful and loud, rising
occasionally into drifting passages of wild melody,
then breaking off into short, melancholy tones, or
sudden shrieks, resembling those of human voices in
distress or pain.

The ice was broken into thousands of confused
shapes, but none, Hans thought, like the ordinary
forms of splintered ice. There seemed a curious
expression about all their outlines — a perpetual
resemblance to living features, distorted and scorn-
ful. Myriads of deceitful shadows, and lurid lights,
played and floated about and through the pale blue
pinnacles, dazzling and confusing the sight of the
traveller; while his ears grew dull and his head giddy
with the constant gush and roar of the concealed
waters. These painful circumstances increased upon
him as he advanced; the ice crashed and yawned
into fresh chasms at his feet, tottering spires nodded
around him, and fell thundering across his path; and
though he had repeatedly faced these dangers on the
most terrific glaciers, and in the wildest weather, it
was with a new and oppressive feeling of panic terror
that he leaped the last chasm, and flung himself,

exhausted and shuddering, on the firm turf of the mountain.

He had been compelled to abandon his basket of food, which became a perilous encumbrance on the glacier, and had now no means of refreshing himself but by breaking off and eating some of the pieces of ice. This, however, relieved his thirst; an hour's repose recruited his hardy frame, and, with the indomitable spirit of avarice, he resumed his laborious journey.

His way now lay straight up a ridge of bare red rocks, without a blade of grass to ease the foot, or a projecting angle to afford an inch of shade from the south sun. It was past noon, and the rays beat intensely upon the steep path, while the whole atmosphere was motionless, and penetrated with heat. Intense thirst was soon added to the bodily fatigue with which Hans was now afflicted; glance after glance he cast on the flask of water which hung at his belt. "Three drops are enough," at last thought he; "I may, at least, cool my lips with it."

He opened the flask, and was raising it to his lips, when his eye fell on an object lying on the rock beside him; he thought it moved. It was a small dog, apparently in the last agony of death from thirst. Its tongue was out, its jaws dry, its limbs extended lifelessly, and a swarm of black ants were crawling about its lips and throat. Its eye moved to the bottle which Hans held in his hand. He raised it, drank, spurned the animal with his foot, and passed on.

And he did not know how it was, but he thought that a strange shadow had suddenly come across the blue sky.

The path became steeper and more rugged every

moment; and the high hill air, instead of refreshing him, seemed to throw his blood into a fever. The noise of the hill cataracts sounded like mockery in his ears: they were all distant, and his thirst increased every moment. Another hour passed, and he again looked down to the flask at his side; it was half empty, but there was much more than three drops in it. He stopped to open it, and again, as he did so, something moved in the path above him. It was a fair child, stretched nearly lifeless on the rock, its breast heaving with thirst, its eyes closed, and its lips parched and burning. Hans eyed it deliberately, drank, and passed on. And a dark grey cloud came over the sun, and long, snake-like shadows crept up along the mountain sides. Hans struggled on. The sun was sinking, but its descent seemed to bring no coolness; the leaden weight of the dead air pressed upon his brow and heart, but the goal was near. He saw the cataract of the Golden River springing from the hill-side, scarcely five hundred feet above him. He paused for a moment to breathe, and sprang on to complete his task.

At this instant a faint cry fell on his ear. He turned, and saw a grey-haired old man extended on the rocks. His eyes were sunk, his features deadly pale, and gathered into an expression of despair. "Water!" he stretched his arms to Hans, and cried feebly, "Water! I am dying."

"I have none," replied Hans; "thou hast had thy share of life." He strode over the prostrate body and darted on. And a flash of blue lightning rose out of the East, shaped like a sword; it shook thrice over the whole heaven, and left it dark with one heavy, impenetrable shade. The sun was setting; it plunged towards the horizon like a red-hot ball.

The roar of the Golden River rose on Hans' ear. He stood at the brink of the chasm through which it

ran. Its waves were filled with the red glory of the
sunset; they shook their crests like tongues of fire,
and flashes of blood-red light gleamed along their
foam. Their sound came mightier and mightier on
his senses; his brain grew giddy with the prolonged
thunder. Shuddering, he drew the flask from his
girdle and hurled it into the centre of the torrent.
As he did so, an icy chill shot through his limbs; he
staggered, shrieked, and fell. The waters closed over
his cry. And the moaning of the river rose wildly
into the night, as it gushed over

THE BLACK STONE.

CHAPTER IV

HOW MR. SCHWARTZ SET OFF ON AN EXPEDITION TO THE GOLDEN RIVER, AND HOW HE PROSPERED THEREIN

OOR little Gluck waited very anxiously alone in the house for Hans' return. Finding he did not come back, he was terribly frightened, and went and told Schwartz in the prison all that had happened. Then Schwartz was very much pleased, and said that Hans must certainly have been turned into a black stone, and he should have all the gold to himself. But Gluck was very sorry, and cried all night. When he got up in the morning, there was no bread in the house, nor any money; so Gluck went and hired himself to another goldsmith, and he worked so hard, and so neatly, and so long every day, that he soon got money enough together to pay his brother's fine, and he went and gave it all to Schwartz, and

Schwartz got out of prison. Then Schwartz was quite
pleased, and said he should have some of the gold
of the river. But Gluck only begged he would go and
see what had become of Hans.

Now when Schwartz had heard that Hans had
stolen the holy water, he thought to himself that
such a proceeding might not be considered altogether
correct by the King of the Golden River, and deter-
mined to manage matters better. So he took some
more of Gluck's money, and went to a bad priest,
who gave him some holy water very readily for it.
Then Schwartz was sure it was all quite right. So
Schwartz got up early in the morning before the sun
rose, and took some bread and wine in a basket,
and put his holy water in a flask, and set off for the
mountains. Like his brother he was much surprised
at the sight of the glacier, and had great difficulty
in crossing it, even after leaving his basket behind
him. The day was cloudless, but not bright: there was
a heavy purple haze hanging over the sky, and the
hills looked lowering and gloomy. And as Schwartz
climbed the steep rock path, the thirst came upon
him, as it had upon his brother, until he lifted his
flask to his lips to drink. Then he saw the fair child
lying near him on the rocks, and it cried to him,
and moaned for water.

"Water, indeed," said Schwartz; "I haven't half
enough for myself," and passed on. And as he went he
thought the sunbeams grew more dim, and he saw
a low bank of black cloud rising out of the West;

and, when he had climbed for another hour, the thirst overcame him again, and he would have drunk. Then he saw the old man lying before him on the path, and heard him cry out for water. "Water, indeed," said Schwartz; "I haven't half enough for myself," and on he went.

Then again the light seemed to fade from before his eyes, and he looked up, and, behold, a mist, of the colour of blood, had come over the sun; and the bank of black cloud had risen very high, and its edges were tossing and tumbling like the waves of the angry sea. And they cast long shadows, which flickered over Schwartz's path.

Then Schwartz climbed for another hour, and again his thirst returned; and as he lifted his flask to his lips, he thought he saw his brother Hans lying

D^{119}

exhausted on the path before him, and, as he gazed, the figure stretched its arms to him, and cried for water. "Ha, ha," laughed Schwartz, "are you there? remember the prison bars, my boy. Water, indeed! do you suppose I carried it all the way up here for *you*?" And he strode over the figure; yet, as he passed, he thought he saw a strange expression of mockery about its lips. And, when he had gone a few yards farther, he looked back; but the figure was not there.

And a sudden horror came over Schwartz, he knew not why; but the thirst for gold prevailed over his fear, and he rushed on. And the bank of black cloud rose to the zenith, and out of it came bursts of spiry lightning, and waves of darkness seemed to heave and float, between their flashes, over the whole heavens. And the sky where the sun was setting was all level, and like a lake of blood; and a strong wind came out of that sky, tearing its crimson clouds into fragments, and scattering them far into the darkness. And when Schwartz stood by the brink of the Golden River, its waves were black, like thunder clouds, but their foam was like fire; and the roar of the waters below and the thunder above met, as he cast the flask into the stream. And, as he did so, the lightning glared in his eyes, and the earth gave way beneath him, and the waters closed over his cry. And the moaning of the river rose wildly into the night, as it gushed over the

Two Black Stones.

CHAPTER V

HEN Gluck found that Schwartz
did not come back, he was
very sorry, and did not know
what to do. He had no money,
and was obliged to go and
hire himself again to the goldsmith, who worked him very
hard, and gave him very little
money. So, after a month,
or two, Gluck grew tired,
and made up his mind to go
and try his fortune with the Golden River. "The
little King looked very kind," thought he. "I don't
think he will turn me into a black stone." So he
went to the priest, and the priest gave him some
holy water as soon as he asked for it. Then Gluck
took some bread in his basket, and the bottle of
water, and set off very early for the mountains.

If the glacier had occasioned a great deal of fatigue
to his brothers, it was twenty times worse for him,
who was neither so strong nor so practised on the

mountains. He had several very bad falls, lost his
basket and bread, and was very much frightened
at the strange noises under the ice. He lay a long
time to rest on the grass, after he had got over, and
began to climb the hill just in the hottest part of the
day. When he had climbed for an hour, he got dread-
fully thirsty, and was going to drink like his brothers,
when he saw an old man coming down the path

above him, looking very feeble, and leaning on a staff.
"My son," said the old man, "I am faint with thirst,
give me some of that water." Then Gluck looked at
him, and when he saw that he was pale and weary,
he gave him the water: "Only pray don't drink it
all," said Gluck. But the old man drank a great deal,
and gave him back the bottle two-thirds empty.
Then he bade him good speed, and Gluck went on
again merrily. And the path became easier to his
feet, and two or three blades of grass appeared upon

it, and some grass-hoppers began sing-ing on the bank beside it; and Gluck thought he had never heard such merry singing.

Then he went on for another hour, and the thirst in-creased on him so that he thought he should be forced to drink. But, as he raised the flask, he saw a little child lying panting by the road-side, and it cried out piteously for water. Then Gluck struggled with himself, and deter-mined to bear the thirst a little longer: and he put the bottle to the child's lips, and it drank it all but a few drops. Then it smiled on him, and got up,

and ran down the hill; and Gluck looked after it,
till it became as small as a little star, and then
turned, and began climbing again. And then there
were all kinds of sweet flowers growing on the rocks,
bright green moss, with pale pink starry flowers,
and soft belled gentians, more blue than the sky
at its deepest, and pure white transparent lilies.
And crimson and purple butterflies darted hither
and thither, and the sky sent down such pure light,
that Gluck had never felt so happy in his life.

Yet, when he had climbed for another hour, his
thirst became intolerable again; and, when he looked
at his bottle, he saw that there were only five or six
drops left in it, and he could not venture to drink.
And, as he was hanging the flask to his belt again, he
saw a little dog lying on the rocks, gasping for breath
—just as Hans had seen it on the day of his ascent.
And Gluck stopped and looked at it, and then at the
Golden River, not five hundred yards above him;
and he thought of the dwarf's words, "that no one
could succeed, except in their first attempt"; and he
tried to pass the dog, but it whined piteously, and
Gluck stopped again. "Poor beastie," said Gluck,
"it'll be dead when I come down again, if I don't
help it." Then he looked closer and closer at it, and
its eye turned on him so mournfully, that he could
not stand it. "Confound the King and his gold too,"
said Gluck; and he opened the flask and poured all
the water into the dog's mouth.

The dog sprang up and stood on its hind legs. Its

tail disappeared, its ears became long, longer, silky, golden; its nose became very red, its eyes became very twinkling; in three seconds the dog was gone, and before Gluck stood his old acquaintance, the King of the Golden River.

"Thank you," said the monarch, "but don't be frightened, it's all right"; for Gluck showed manifest symptoms of consternation at this unlooked-for reply to his last observation. "Why didn't you come before," continued the dwarf, "instead of sending me those rascally brothers of yours, for me to have the trouble of turning into stones? Very hard stones they make too."

"Oh dear me!" said Gluck, "have you really been so cruel?"

"Cruel!" said the dwarf, "they poured unholy water into my stream: do you suppose I'm going to allow that?"

"Why," said Gluck, "I am sure, sir—your majesty, I mean—they got the water out of the church font."

"Very probably," replied the dwarf; "but," and his countenance grew stern as he spoke, "the water which has been refused to the cry of the weary and dying is unholy, though it had been blessed by every saint in heaven; and the water which is found in the vessel of mercy is holy, though it had been defiled with corpses."

So saying, the dwarf stooped and plucked a lily that grew at his feet. On its white leaves there hung three drops of clear dew. And the dwarf shook them

into the flask which Gluck held in his hand. "Cast
these into the river," he said, "and descend on the
other side of the mountains into the Treasure Valley.
And so good speed."

As he spoke, the figure of the dwarf became in-
distinct. The playing colours of his robe formed themselves into a prismatic mist of dewy light: he stood
for an instant veiled with them as with the belt of a
broad rainbow. The colours grew faint, the mist rose
into the air; the monarch had evaporated.

And Gluck climbed to the brink of the Golden
River, and its waves were as clear as crystal, and as
brilliant as the sun. And, when he cast the three
drops of dew into the stream, there opened where
they fell a small circular whirlpool, into which the
waters descended with a musical noise. Gluck stood
watching it for some time, very much disappointed,
because not only the river was not turned into gold,
but its waters seemed much diminished in quantity.
Yet he obeyed his friend the dwarf, and descended
the other side of the mountains, towards the Treasure
Valley; and, as he went, he thought he heard the noise
of water working its way under the ground. And,
when he came in sight of the Treasure Valley, behold,
a river, like the Golden River, was springing from a
new cleft of the rocks above it, and was flowing in
innumerable streams among the dry heaps of red
sand. And as Gluck gazed, fresh grass sprang beside
the new streams, and creeping plants grew, and
climbed among the moistening soil. Young flowers

opened suddenly along the river sides, as stars leap
out when twilight is deepening, and thickets of
myrtle, and tendrils of vine, cast lengthening shadows
over the valley as they grew. And thus the Treasure
Valley became a garden again, and the inheritance,
which had been lost by cruelty, was regained by love.
And Gluck went and dwelt in the valley, and the
poor were never driven from his door; so that his
barns became full of corn, and his house of treasure.
And, for him, the river had, according to the dwarf's
promise, become a River of Gold. And, to this day,
the inhabitants of the valley point to the place where
the three drops of holy dew were cast into the stream,
and trace the course of the Golden River under the
ground, until it emerges in the Treasure Valley. And,
at the top of the cataract of the Golden River, are
still to be seen two BLACK STONES, round which the
waters howl mournfully every day at sunset; and
these stones are still called by the people of the valley,

THE BLACK BROTHERS.

Some stories are not worth a second reading, but *The King of the Golden River* is not one of them. Let us think it over:

Chapter I. Was it really good farming to shoot the blackbirds, kill the hedgehogs, poison the crickets, and smother the cicadas? Perhaps you can find a picture of a cicada in some big book at home or in the library and make a sketch of one.

The little old gentleman is very carefully described. I wonder if the clever artist who drew the first picture has got the details right. You could make a good scene for a play from part of this Chapter. Begin with "Hollo!" on page 18 and end with "a tremendous rap at the door" on page 21. In fact the whole Chapter could be acted, with some parts missed out, of course. Which part would *you* like to act? Examine each picture as you go along to see if it goes exactly with the story. What an excellent film this Chapter would make! Why does South West Wind, Esquire, have a nose like a trumpet? Try to make a sketch of his visiting-card.

Chapter II. Some of the words and phrases are rather grand— "abandoned their valueless patrimony in despair," "gaining a livelihood," and so on; but it is not very hard to see what they mean so long as you do not split them up into single words. It is worth while trying to make a sketch of that mug, following the description, "The handle was . . . circumference." Why had Schwartz seen the mug's eyes wink?

What a lovely coloured picture of the mountain tops Gluck saw as he looked disconsolately from the window, and how lovely are the words which describe it, especially if you read them aloud very softly and carefully! Do you know anyone with a *metallic* voice? And you know what an effervescent drink is; but what is an effervescent melody? Can you find the *crucible* in one of the pictures? If you had some gold paint, where would you use it in the picture of Gluck and the dwarf? I wonder how tall Gluck was?

What tremendous words!—"inclining to coppery in complexion, and indicative, in expression, of a very pertinacious and intractable disposition in their small proprietor." I wonder what it means in your own language? The dwarf of a foot and a half high took two turns of three feet long and then six feet long! But then, of course, he was a King and could take strides as long as he chose. He was fortunately not a very ceremonious monarch or he might have objected to Gluck asking him whether he had once been a mug. Of course you know that holy water was water that the priest had blessed. What a picture there is in the description of the King's disappearance! Is there any resemblance between South West Wind, Esquire, and H.M. the King of the Golden River?

CHAPTER III.

It is wonderful how the hard words become easy if you read the whole paragraph straight on, not *too* quickly, of course, instead of making hurdles of single words — for example, "the steadiness with which he adhered to his story obtained him some degree of credence."

What do you think of the magistrate's court in the little picture? If you are "an abandoned character" you cannot expect to get favours from priests or anyone else; and not even your companion in abandonment is of any service to you. It is such a relief to turn from Hans and Schwartz to the lovely coloured picture which begins at "Level lines of dewy mist," and ends with "peaks of the eternal snow," and which reads rather like poetry.

And then a special paragraph for a description of the Golden River itself! There is a good "*sound*-picture" in the passage, "The ice was excessively slippery . . . in distress or pain."

What was it which made Hans persevere so pluckily? Hans had his good points like all other bad men, but instead of turning *outwards* to defend him they turned *inwards* and hurt himself. Note the three varied effects of Hans' unkindness:

Dog—a strange shadow across the blue sky.

Child . . .?

Old man . . .?

We call the end of a story like this the climax or crisis. It is a terrible one for Hans!

Of course Gluck had no real reason to be sorry
CHAPTER IV.   that Hans had not returned, except
one which you can probably guess
for yourself. As for his treatment of Schwartz,
it seems almost too good to be true, and reminds
us of the higher law of which we read in the New
Testament: "But I say unto you, Love your..."
Perhaps you can finish the sentence?

In what way was Schwartz an improvement upon
Hans in making preparations for his journey? Had
he a good motive for not stealing the holy water,
and was it *very* much better to buy it? He was sure,
however, that "it was all quite right." Probably he
thought that everything he did was "all quite right."
If so, that was the worst thing about him.

How did the journey of Schwartz differ from that
of his brother? And how do the two descriptions
differ? Did Schwartz really see Hans?

Try to sketch *two* Black Stones to go at the end
of this Chapter.

You will probably feel that you could write this
CHAPTER V.   Chapter yourself, or at all events tell
shortly what there is sure to be in it.
But read carefully, all the same, and find out exactly
how the author works it all out.

The terror of the glacier had not been merely
imagined by Hans and Schwartz. It was just as real
for Gluck. What was the *immediate* effect of his

kindness to the old man? (It is expressed in one word ending in -ly.)

Why did the old man say "My son" to Gluck, and not to either of his brothers?

Try to put into verses the description beginning, "And there were all kinds of sweet flowers . . ."

What is the surprise in this Chapter?

What are "manifest symptoms of consternation"?

How would *you* have finished the story? Would you have brought Hans and Schwartz back to life again? Does gold play a large part or a small part in this story? In what sense had the river become a River of Gold?

What are the qualities which the author of this story asks us to admire?

What are the faults which he expects us to condemn?

THE WRITER OF "THE KING OF THE GOLDEN RIVER"

His name was John Ruskin, and though he lived as long as eighty-one years, he was always about the same age as Peter Pan, which is probably about your own age. He wrote many wise books, but none of them were wiser than *The King of the Golden River*, for though he invented all the *facts* of that story, he did not invent the lovely idea of it, which is not "as old as the hills," but very much older, and many times more lasting. He was born in 1819, and died in 1900, but these dates do not really matter, and you are quite welcome to forget them if you choose, so long as you do not turn them topsy-turvy.

Now these were the rules of the mother of John Ruskin, and they were very strictly kept:

1. Boys and girls who insist upon having their own way must be prepared to take the consequences.

[On one occasion the consequence of wilfully touching and persisting in touching a tea-urn on the breakfast table was a burnt finger.]

2. No toys allowed.

[A kind aunt brought home a Punch and Judy when John Ruskin was a child, but he was not allowed to play with it!]

3. The Bible must be read every day; and no chapter must be missed, not even if it is full of long and difficult names.

4. A good whipping is the best cure for ill temper.

You may think that John Ruskin had a very unhappy childhood, but he would have told you that it was quite otherwise. He learnt the lesson of the tea-urn and never forgot it all his life. As a tiny child he enjoyed the jingle of his mother's keys as much as another child enjoyed the most expensive silver and coral rattle. When he could not get toy bricks to play with he counted those in the wall over the way, and took great delight in a water-cart which was filled from an iron post near his mother's front door. After a time he enjoyed the Bible readings, and the glorious language of the Old Book helped more than anything else to make him an author. And he lived to thank his mother for the whippings which prevented him from growing up ill-tempered, selfish and greedy. So all was well that ended well; besides, he knew that if he were ever sick or sad it was his mother who would nurse and comfort him.

Though John Ruskin lived in London he did not stay there all the time. He was often taken to the country for the fresh air, and a little later he went with his father and mother to Scotland, travelling by sea. At Perth he met a girl cousin with whom he had many a merry game in a garden at the foot of which there was a door which, when you opened it, let you out on the bank of the River Tay.

And far beyond the river were the mountains, blue
in the distance—you know from *The King of the
Golden River* how John Ruskin loved the mountains.
When a famous artist named Northcote painted his
portrait he asked the little sitter what he should paint
in the background, and the child answered promptly,
"Blue hills."

Then came learning to read. His mother was his
teacher, and began with syllables. But these had no
meaning to John, who read whole sentences at a
time and then went back to study the single words.
As we have already seen, this is the best way to read
his story.

After that came the tours! How would you like
to set out in the springtime in a big roomy coach,
made as comfortable inside as a drawing-room, and
go galloping away in the sunshine into half the
counties of England and some of those of Wales,
and at times into Scotland as well?

The roads were in good order, for railways had not
yet been made, and the chariot would run smoothly
along until it reached a well-kept inn. Then as it
rattled under the archway into the cobbled stable-
yard little John would hear the call "Horses out,"
and in a few minutes fresh horses would come
prancing from the stables to be harnessed to the
chariot. Then the post-boy who drove them would
crack his whip and the family would go on again as
merrily as before—for both John's parents travelled
with him on these jolly journeys.

At times the journey was broken to allow the travellers to see some old castle or great house with a gallery full of beautiful pictures, or to wander about through the streets of an interesting old town to see the shops or to visit some grand cathedral.

Then there was the wonderful postillion's whip mounted with silver which was made for John, so that he could ride on his father's legs in the chariot and make those willing horses go faster and faster.

Year after year these "worshipful pilgrimages" were repeated, and John Ruskin learnt more from them than he ever learnt from tutors or even from books. Fancy learning the geography of your own country by visiting all its varied scenes and seeing things with your own eyes instead of reading about them!

Then the Ruskins went to live at Herne Hill, which is now part of London, with railways and trams and motor-buses, but was then really in the country. Here he had a garden to roam about in which he never forgot, for he wrote about it in his old age.

The first joy of the year being its snowdrops, the second and cardinal one, was in the almond blossom— every other garden and woodland gladness following from that in an unbroken order of kindling flower and shadowy leaf; and for many and many a year to come —until, indeed, the whole of life became autumn to me —my chief prayer for the kindness of heaven, in its flowerful seasons, was that the frost might not touch the almond blossom.

When John Ruskin was writing the book which
contains the above words, he laid down his pen and
took up the Bible which he had used in his childhood, and as he opened it a paper dropped from it
which he had not seen for a lifetime, and which
contained a list of the chapters he had been required
to learn by heart. You may perhaps be sufficiently
interested to look up some of them—say:

> Exodus, chaps. xv. and xx.
> 1 Kings, chap. viii.
> Psalms xxiii., xxxii., xc., ciii.
> Proverbs, chaps. ii., iii., viii. and xii.
> Isaiah, chap. lviii.
> Matthew, chaps. v., vi. and vii.
> 1 Corinthians, chaps. xiii. and xv.
> Revelation, chaps. v. and vi.

He calls this Bible reading "the most precious and
on the whole the most essential part of his education."

The boy had not nearly so many books as you
can get, but one was Pope's translation of Homer, and
he had also a few of the novels of Sir Walter Scott.
The latter were used during the family visits to
Scotland. If the way lay near Melrose he would read
The Monastery, if near Kinross and Loch Leven,
The Abbot, and so on, for in this way he could live
over again the incidents described by the novelist,
could see Queen Mary come down one dark night
from a door in the old castle wall to the shore of the
island and watch her being rowed swiftly and silently
across the dark waters of the loch. It was not sufficient

for him to read a book. Anyone can do that. He must *see*, with the mind's eye, all the pen-pictures drawn by the writer and throw himself into one character after the other so that they lived again in his own person.

As for poetry, the boy learnt to love it, not by reading the many books on the shelves, but by hearing his father read aloud some of the finest passages of Shakespeare, Spenser, Goldsmith, Byron, Scott, and many another who could produce

The long resounding march and melody divine.

He lived in a home of peace.

I never heard [he writes] my father's or my mother's voice once raised in any question with each other; nor have seen an angry, or even slightly hurt or offended glance in the eyes of either. I had never heard a servant scolded, nor even suddenly, passionately, or in any severe manner, blamed. I had never seen a moment's trouble or disorder in any household matter; nor anything whatever either done in a hurry, or undone in due time. . . .

Next to this quite priceless gift of Peace, I had received the perfect understanding of the natures of Obedience and Faith. I obeyed word or lifted finger of father and mother, simply as a ship her helm. . . . And my practice in Faith was soon complete: nothing was ever promised me that was not given: nothing ever threatened me that was not inflicted; and nothing ever told me that was not true.

Peace, obedience, faith; these three for chief good; next to these the habit of fixed attention with both eyes and mind.

The boy was very young when he first began to write, and he had quite made up his mind to be an author and to write many books of great length. The days were much too short, for he was not only learning Greek, Latin, French, drawing, arithmetic and geology, but writing a story which was to appear in four volumes (rather small indeed), to be called *Harry and Lucy Concluded; or Early Lessons*, and to be illustrated by the author. I expect you would call it "goody-goody," or "slow." Here are the first lines of a poem written about the same time, and called *The Needless Alarm*:

Among the rushes lived a mouse
with a pretty little house
made of rushes tall and high
that to the skies were heard to sigh
while one night while she was sleeping
comes a dog that then was peeping
and has found her out in spite
of her good wall for then his sight
was better than our mouse's.

We must give the little seven-year-old poet good marks for rhyme, and Alpha Plus for the fourth line. I wonder why? Some day you may find out who saved the mouse.

The poet must have felt greatly encouraged by his first try, for he took a long and deep breath and set himself to do next *A Poem of the Universe*! He reached the middle of the second volume before he found out that the subject was really too big; perhaps it was Cousin Mary from Perth who had something to do with it.

She was fourteen, which is rather old, and only a
girl, and he was ten and a poet, but she was ever so
much better than loneliness, and besides she took
turn about in the long Bible readings! which were
still steadily continued. Much better were the long
journeys in the chariot now that Mary shared them.
Moreover she kept a diary like her boy cousin, and
it was great good fun to read them over when they
came back to Herne Hill. (Did I say that was the name
of the country place near London where the Ruskins
lived? I forget.)

Then came the delightful Mondays, Wednesdays
and Fridays when John read Greek odes with Dr.
Andrews, for college life at Oxford was drawing near.
You would have loved to be taught by Dr. Andrews.
"He is so funny," wrote the delighted pupil, "com-
paring Neptune's lifting up of the wrecked ships
of Æneas with his trident to my lifting up a potato
with a fork or taking a piece of bread out of a bowl
of milk with a spoon." But the grammar was not
very well done, for grammar will have nothing to do
with fun about potatoes; it is much too dignified,
as you know very well.

John Ruskin was to become famous as an author,
but it is difficult to explain what kind of an author
he was going to be. However, as his first great book
was about artists and their works, and especially
about a great English artist named Turner, it is interesting to learn a little about his first introduction to
art. Mary had drawing lessons at school, and tried

to draw some of the things and places which she saw
from the chariot on the summer tours. Her work
did not satisfy John, so he took drawing lessons
himself, and learnt also how to use colour. He had
a great love for fine buildings, and one of his first
drawings showed the main tower of Canterbury
Cathedral. Then on his thirteenth birthday he received as a gift a copy of a book on Italy, illustrated
by Turner. Later his father brought home another
book called *Sketches in Flanders and Germany*, from
drawings made by an artist named Prout, and this
book was a source of great delight. As the boy and
his father pored (do you ever pore?) over it Mrs.
Ruskin said quietly, "Why not go and see the places
shown in the pictures?" It seemed for a moment too
good to be true, but the idea was carried out in the
following spring, to the boy's intense delight. Who
would *not* have been delighted? To go off into foreign
lands with a courier bearing a splendid name like
Salvador and travel about in a coach at a pace which
allowed time to see things at leisure; a coach which
could be stopped when the travellers so desired in
order to allow them to "stand and stare." John
Ruskin hated railways to the end of his days, for he
objected to be sent through the country "like a
parcel," and he would have hated motor cars still
more, for he loved to "go there" rather than merely
to "get there"—two very different things.

They crossed to Calais and "posted" to Brussels
and Cologne, and then went up the Rhine to Stras-

bourg (a map would help you here). Then they moved on to Schaffhausen, and on Sunday went out for a quiet walk beyond the town.

Here [Ruskin wrote afterwards] we were high above the River Rhine and had a wide view, both to the south and the west, of the open country. . . . At which open country, of low undulation, far into blue—gazing as at one of our own distances from Malvern of Worcester-shire, or Dorking of Kent—suddenly—behold—beyond.

There was no thought in any of us for a moment of their being clouds. They were clear as crystal, sharp on the pure horizon sky, and already tinged with rose by the sinking sun. Infinitely beyond all that we had ever thought or dreamed—the seen walls of lost Eden could not have been more beautiful to us; not more awful round Heaven the walls of sacred death.

What had he seen? The Alps.

I went down that evening [he goes on] with my destiny fixed in all of it that was to be sacred and useful.

Strange words, you may think, but some day you will learn from *Modern Painters* and other books of this author a little of what the Alps meant to Ruskin.

Home again and serious work, now at King's College, London, in preparation for Oxford, for the boy was now seventeen. Then came Adèle Domecq with her two sisters, beautiful and lively girls, the daughters of Mr. Ruskin's partner, and with Adèle John fell in love. He wrote stories and poems for her, but she only laughed merrily at him. And that was hard to bear. But when she went back to her father's

house in Paris, his attention was diverted by the
preparation for Oxford, and one autumn morning he
drove away with his father and was entered as a
Gentleman Commoner. "I remember still as if it
were yesterday," he wrote in his old age, "the pride
of first walking out of the Angel Hotel and past
University College, holding my father's arm, in my
velvet cap and silk gown." In the following January
he began his college life.

His boyhood was over and three years' hard work
before him. He was *rather* lonely on that first evening,
alone by his own fireside, but after sitting before the
fire for a time he "said his prayers very seriously
and went to bed in good hope." At first he was equally
lonely when he dined in the great hall of the college
among what seemed to be a countless number of
students, and thought of the comfortable midday
meal with his mother and Mary in the small parlour
at home.

But before long he made friends and settled down
to serious work. His mother took lodgings in Oxford,
and his father came down from London at the week-
ends. He passed his first examinations and gained a
prize for a poem, to the delight of his parents and
himself. Then for a year he worked very hard, so
hard indeed that when he heard that Adèle Domecq
had married he had a breakdown in health, and was
ordered complete rest and change. For a year he
travelled abroad, but he did not get well very quickly,
though when he left Italy and came again within

sight of the Swiss mountains he began once more to take an interest in life.

On reaching home he spent a great deal of his time in drawing and studying geology. At this time his mother had a visitor, a young girl from Scotland, who was much amused at his devotion to his studies, and suggested that he should, as a relaxation, write a fairy story. The remark was obviously made in fun, but the student took it seriously and set to work. The result was *The King of the Golden River*, which has given delight to many thousands since it was read to the girl who suggested its composition.

And the rest will keep until later.

OTHER GOLDEN STORIES

THE GOLDEN GOOSE

THERE was a man who had three sons. The youngest was called Dummling—which is much the same as Dunderhead, for all thought he was more than half a fool—and he was at all times mocked and ill-treated by the whole household.

It happened that the eldest son took it into his head one day to go into the wood to cut fuel; and his mother gave him a nice pasty and a bottle of wine to take with him, that he might refresh himself at his work. As he went into the wood, a little old man bid him good day, and said, "Give me a little piece of meat from your plate, and a little wine out of your bottle, for I am very hungry and thirsty." But this clever young man said, "Give you my meat and wine? No, I thank you, I should not have enough left for myself": and away he went. He soon began to cut down a tree; but he had not worked long before he missed his stroke and cut himself, and was forced to go home to have the wound dressed. Now it was the little old man that sent him this mischief.

Next went out the second son to work: and his mother gave him also a pasty and a bottle of wine. And the same little old man met him also, and asked him for something to eat and drink. But he too thought himself very clever, and said, "The more you eat the less there would be for me: so go your

77

way!" The little man took care that he too should
have his reward, and the second stroke that he aimed
against a tree hit him on the leg; so that he too was
forced to go home.

Then Dummling said, "Father, I should like to go
and cut wood too." But his father said, "Your
brothers have both lamed themselves; you had better
stay at home, for you know nothing about the business of wood-cutting." But Dummling was very
pressing; and at last his father said, "Go your way!
you will be wiser when you have smarted for your
folly." And his mother gave him only some dry
bread and a bottle of sour beer. But when he went
into the wood, he met the little old man, who said,
"Give me some meat and drink, for I am very hungry
and thirsty." Dummling said, "I have only dry bread
and sour beer; if that will suit you, we will sit down
and eat it, such as it is, together." So they sat down;
and when the lad pulled out his bread, behold it was
turned into a rich pasty: and his sour beer, when they
tasted it, was delightful wine. They ate and drank
heartily; and when they had done, the little man
said, "As you have a kind heart, and have been
willing to share everything with me, I will send a
blessing upon you. There stands an old tree; cut it
down, and you will find something at the root."
Then he took his leave and went his way.

Dummling set to work, and cut down the tree;
and when it fell, he found, in a hollow under the roots,
a goose with feathers of pure gold. He took it up, and

went on to a little inn by the roadside, where he thought to sleep for the night on his way home. Now the landlord had three daughters; and when they saw the goose they were very eager to discover what this wonderful bird could be, and wished very much to pluck one of the feathers out of its tail. At last the eldest said, "I must and will have a feather." So she waited till Dummling was gone to bed, and then seized the goose by the wing; but to her great wonder there she stuck, for neither hand nor finger could she get away again. Then in came the second sister, and thought to have a feather too; but the moment she touched her sister, there she too hung fast. At last came the third, and she also wanted a feather; but the other two cried out, "Keep away! for Heaven's sake, keep away!" However, she did not understand what they meant. "If they are there," thought she, "I may as well be there too." So she went up to them; but the moment she touched her sisters she stuck fast, and hung to the goose as they did. And so they kept company with the goose all night in the cold.

The next morning Dummling got up and carried off the goose under his arm. He took no notice at all of the three girls, but went out with them sticking fast behind. So wherever he travelled, they too were forced to follow, whether they would or no, as fast as their legs could carry them.

In the middle of a field the parson met them; and when he saw the train, he said, "Are you not ashamed of yourselves, you bold girls, to run after a young

man in that way over the fields? Is that good behaviour?" Then he took the youngest by the hand
to lead her away; but as soon as he touched her he
too hung fast, and followed in the train; though
sorely against his will, for he was not only in rather
too good plight for running fast, but just then he
had a little touch of the gout in the great toe of his
right foot. By and by up came the clerk; and when
he saw his master, the parson, running after the three
girls, he wondered greatly and said, "Holla! holla!
your reverence! whither so fast? there is a christening
to-day." Then he ran up and took him by the gown;
when, lo and behold, he stuck fast too. As the five
were thus trudging along, one behind another, they
met two labourers with their mattocks coming from
work; and the parson cried out lustily to them to
help him. But scarcely had they laid hands on
him, when they too fell into the rank; and so they
made seven, all running together after Dummling
and his goose.

Now Dummling thought he would see a little of
the world before he went home; so he and his train
journeyed on, till at last they came to a city where
there was a king who had an only daughter. The
princess was of so thoughtful and moody a turn of
mind that no one could make her laugh; and the king
had made known to all the world, that whoever could
make her laugh should have her for his wife. When
the young man heard this, he went to her, with his
goose and all its train; and as soon as she saw the

seven all hanging together, and running along, treading on each other's heels, she could not help bursting into a long and loud laugh. Then Dummling claimed her for his wife, and married her; and he was heir to the kingdom, and lived long and happily with his wife.

But what became of the goose and the goose's tail I never could hear.

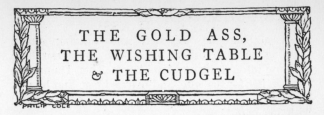

THE GOLD ASS,
THE WISHING TABLE
& THE CUDGEL

A LONG time ago there lived a tailor who had three sons but only one goat. As the goat supplied the whole family with milk, she had to be well fed and taken daily to pasture. This the sons did in turn. One day the eldest son led her into the churchyard, where he knew there was fine herbage to be found, and there let her browse and skip about till evening. It being then time to return home, he said to her, "Goat, have you had enough to eat?" and the goat answered:

> *"I have eaten so much*
> *Not a leaf can I touch, Dan, Dan."*

"Come along home then," said the boy, and he led her by the cord round her neck back to the stable and tied her up.

"Well," said the old tailor, "has the goat had her proper amount of food?"

"Why, she has eaten so much, not a leaf can she touch," answered the son.

The father, however, thinking he should like to assure himself of this, went down to the stable, patted the animal and said caressingly, "Goat, have you really had enough to eat?" The goat answered:

> *"How can my hunger be allayed?*
> *About the little graves I played*
> *And could not find a single blade, Dan, Dan."*

"What is this I hear!" cried the tailor, and running upstairs to his son, "You young liar!" he exclaimed, "to tell me the goat had had enough to eat, and all the while she is starving." And overcome with anger, he took his yard-measure down from the wall and beat his son out of doors.

The next day it was the second son's turn, and he found a place near the garden hedge, where there were the juiciest plants for the goat to feed upon, and she enjoyed them so much that she ate them all up. Before taking her home in the evening, he said to her, "Goat, have you had enough to eat?" and the goat answered:

> *"I have eaten so much*
> *Not a leaf can I touch, Dan, Dan."*

"Come along home then," said the boy, and he led her away to the stable and tied her up.

"Well," said the old tailor, "has the goat had her proper amount of food?"

"Why, she has eaten so much, not a leaf can she touch," answered the boy.

But the tailor was not satisfied with this, and went down to the stable. "Goat, have you really had enough to eat?" he asked; and the goat answered:

> *"How can my hunger be allayed?*
> *About the little graves I played*
> *And could not find a single blade, Dan, Dan.'*

"The shameless young rascal!" cried the tailor, "to let an innocent animal like this starve!" and he ran upstairs, and drove the boy from the house with the yard-measure.

It was now the third son's turn, who, hoping to make things better for himself, let the goat feed on the leaves of all the shrubs he could pick out that were covered with the richest foliage. "Goat, have you had enough to eat?" he said, as the evening fell; and the goat answered:

> *"I have eaten so much*
> *Not a leaf can I touch, Dan, Dan."*

"Come along home then," said the boy, and he took her back and tied her up.

"Well," said the old tailor, "has the goat had her proper amount of food?"

"Why, she has eaten so much, not a leaf can she touch," answered the boy.

But the tailor felt mistrustful, and went down, and asked, "Goat, have you really had enough to eat?" and the mischievous animal answered:

> *"How can my hunger be allayed?*
> *About the little graves I played*
> *And could not find a single blade, Dan, Dan."*

"Oh! what a pack of liars!" cried the tailor; "One as wicked and deceitful as the other; but they shall not make a fool of me any longer." And beside himself with anger, he rushed upstairs, and so belaboured his son with the yard-measure, that the boy fled from the house.

The old tailor was now left alone with his goat. The following morning he went down to the stable

and stroked and caressed her. "Come along, my
pet," he said, "I will take you out myself to-day,"
and he led her by the green hedgerows and weed-
grown banks, and wherever he knew that goats love
to feed. "You shall eat to your heart's content for
once," he said to her, and so let her browse till evening. "Goat, have you had enough to eat?" he asked
her at the close of the day; and she answered:

> *"I have eaten so much*
> *Not a leaf can I touch, Dan, Dan."*

"Come along home then," said the tailor, and he
led her to the stable and tied her up. He turned round,
however, before leaving her, and said once more,
"You have really had enough to eat for once?" But
the goat gave him no better answer than her usual
one, and replied:

> *"How can my hunger be allayed?*
> *About the little graves I played*
> *And could not find a single blade, Dan, Dan."*

On hearing this, the tailor stood, struck dumb with
astonishment. He saw now how unjust he had been
in driving away his sons. When he found his voice,
he cried: "Wait, you ungrateful creature! it is not
enough to drive you away, but I will put such a
mark upon you, that you will not dare to show your
face again among honest tailors." And so saying, he
sprang upstairs, brought down his razor, lathered
the goat's head all over, and shaved it till it was as
smooth as the back of his hand. Then he fetched the

whip,—his yard-measure he considered was too good for such work,—and dealt the animal such blows, that she leapt into the air and away.

Sitting now quite alone in his house, the tailor fell into great melancholy, and would gladly have had his sons back again, but no one knew what had become of them.

The eldest had apprenticed himself to a joiner, and had set himself cheerfully and diligently to learn his trade. When the time came for him to start as a journeyman, his master made him a present of a table, which was of ordinary wood, and to all outward appearance exactly like any other table. It had, however, one good quality, for if anyone set it down, and said, "Table, serve up a meal," it was immediately covered with a nice fresh cloth, laid with a plate, knife and fork, and dishes of boiled and baked meats, as many as there was room for, and a glass of red wine, which only to look at made the heart rejoice.

"I have enough now to last me as long as I live," thought the young man to himself, and accordingly he went about enjoying himself, not minding whether the inns he stayed at were good or bad, whether there was food to be had there or not. Sometimes it pleased him not to seek shelter within them at all, but to turn into a field or a wood, or wherever else he fancied. When there he put down his table, and said, "Serve up a meal," and he was at once supplied with everything he could desire in the way of food.

After he had been going about like this for some

time, he bethought him that he should like to go home again. His father's anger would by this time have passed away, and now that he had the wishing table with him, he was sure of a ready welcome.

He happened, on his homeward way, to come one evening to an inn full of guests. They bid him welcome, and invited him to sit down with them and share their supper, otherwise, they added, he would have a difficulty in getting anything to eat.

But the joiner replied, "I will not take from you what little you have, I would rather that you should consent to be my guests," whereupon they all laughed, thinking he was only joking with them. He now put down his table in the middle of the room, and said, "Table, serve up a meal," and in a moment it was covered with a variety of food of better quality than any the host could have supplied, and a fragrant steam rose from the dishes and greeted the nostrils of the guests. "Now, friends, fall to," said the young man, and the guests, seeing that the invitation was well intended, did not wait to be asked twice, but drew up their chairs and began vigorously to ply their knives and forks. What astonished them most was the way in which, as soon as a dish was empty, another full one appeared in its place. Meanwhile the landlord was standing in the corner of the room looking on; he did not know what to think of it all, but said to himself, "I could make good use of a cook like that."

The joiner and his friends kept up their merriment

late into the night, but at last they retired to rest, the young journeyman placing his table against the wall before going to bed.

The landlord, however, could not sleep for thinking of what he had seen; at last it occurred to him that up in his lumber-room he had an old table which was just such another one to all appearance as the wishing table; so he crept away softly to fetch it, and put it against the wall in place of the other.

When the morning came, the joiner paid for his night's lodging, took up his table, and left, never suspecting that the one he was carrying was not his own.

He reached home at mid-day, and was greeted with joy by his father. "And now, dear son," said the old man, "what trade have you learnt?"

"I am a joiner, father."

"A capital business," responded the father; "and what have you brought home with you from your travels?"

"The best thing I have brought with me, father, is that table."

The tailor carefully examined the table on all sides. "Well," he said at last, "you have certainly not brought a masterpiece back with you; it is a wretched, badly-made old table."

"But it is a wishing table," interrupted his son; "if I put it down and order a meal, it is at once covered with the best of food and wine. If you will only invite your relations and friends, they shall, for once in their lives, have a good meal, for no one ever leaves this table unsatisfied."

When the guests were all assembled, he put his table down as usual, and said, "Table, serve up a meal," but the table did not stir, and remained as empty as any ordinary table at such a command. Then the poor young man saw that his table had been changed, and he was covered with shame at having to stand there before them all like a liar. The guests made fun of him, and had to return home without bite or sup. The tailor took out his cloth and sat down once more to his tailoring, and the son started work again under a master-joiner.

The second son had apprenticed himself to a miller. When his term of apprenticeship had expired, the miller said to him, "As you have behaved so well, I will make you a present of an ass; it is a curious animal; it will neither draw a cart nor carry a sack."

"Of what use is he, then?" asked the young apprentice. "He gives gold," answered the miller; "if you stand him on a cloth, and say 'Bricklebrit,' gold pieces will fall from his mouth."

"That is a handsome present," said the young miller, and he thanked his master and departed.

After this, whenever he was in need of money, he had only to say "Bricklebrit," and a shower of gold pieces fell on the ground, and all he had to do was to pick them up. He ordered the best of everything wherever he went; in short, the dearer the better, for his purse was always full.

He had been going about the world like this for some time, when he began to think he should like to see his father again. "When he sees my gold ass," he said to himself, "he will forget his anger, and be glad to have me back."

It came to pass that he arrived one evening at the same inn in which his brother had had his table stolen from him. He was leading his ass up to the door, when the landlord came out and offered to take the animal, but the young miller refused his help. "Do not trouble yourself," he said; "I will take my old Greycoat myself to the stable and fasten her up, as I like to know where she is."

The landlord was very much astonished at this; the man cannot be very well off, he thought, to look after his own ass. When the stranger, therefore, pulled two gold pieces out of his pocket, and ordered the best of everything that could be got in the market, the landlord opened his eyes, but he ran off with alacrity to do his bidding.

Having finished his meal, the stranger asked for his bill, and the landlord thinking he might safely overcharge such a rich customer, asked for two more gold pieces. The miller felt in his pocket, but found he had spent all his gold. "Wait a minute," he said to the landlord, "I will go and fetch some more money." Whereupon he went out, carrying the table-cloth with him.

This was more than the landlord's curiosity could stand, and he followed his guest to the stable. As the latter bolted the door after him, he went and peeped through a hole in the wall, and there he saw the stranger spread the cloth under his ass, and heard him say "Bricklebrit," and immediately the floor was covered with gold pieces, which fell from the animal's mouth.

"A good thousand, I declare," cried the host; "the gold pieces do not take long to coin! It's not a bad thing to have a money-bag like that."

The guest settled his account and went to bed. During the night the landlord crept down to the stable, led away the gold-coining ass, and fastened up another in its place.

Early the next morning the young miller went off with his ass, thinking all the time that he was leading his own. By noonday he had reached home, where his father gave him a warm welcome.

"What have you been doing with yourself, my son?" asked the old man.

"I am a miller, dear father," he answered.

"And what have you brought home with you from your travels?"

"Nothing but an ass, father."

"There are asses enough here," said the father, "I should have been better pleased if it had been a goat."

"Very likely," replied the son, "but this is no ordinary ass, as it is an ass that coins money; if I say 'Bricklebrit' to it, a whole sackful of gold pours from its mouth. Call all your relations and friends together; I will turn you all into rich people."

"I shall like that well enough," said the tailor, "for then I shall not have to go on plaguing myself with stitching," and he ran out himself to invite his neighbours. As soon as they were all assembled, the young miller asked them to clear a space, and he then spread his cloth and brought the ass into the room. "Now see," said he, and cried "Bricklebrit," but not a single gold piece appeared, and it was evident that the animal knew nothing of the art of gold-coining, for it is not every ass that attains to such a degree of excellence.

The poor young miller pulled a long face, for he saw that he had been tricked: he begged forgiveness of the company, who all returned home as poor as they came. There was nothing to be done now but for the old man to go back to his needle, and the young one to hire himself to a miller.

The third son had apprenticed himself to a turner, which, being a trade requiring a great deal of skill, obliged him to serve a longer time than his brothers. He had, however, heard from them by letter, and knew how badly things had gone with them, and that they had been robbed of their property by an innkeeper on the last evening before reaching home.

When it was time for him to start as a journeyman, his master, being pleased with his conduct, presented him with a bag, saying as he did so, "You will find a cudgel inside."

"The bag I can carry over my shoulder, and it will no doubt be of great service to me, but of what use is a cudgel inside? it will only add to the weight."

"I will explain," said the master. "If any one at any time should behave badly to you, you have only to say, 'Cudgel, out of the bag,' and the stick will jump out, and give him such a cudgelling that he will not be able to move or stir for a week afterwards, and it will not leave off till you say, 'Cudgel, into the bag.'"

The young man thanked him, hung the bag on his back, and when any one threatened to attack him, or in any way to do him harm, he called out, "Cudgel, out of the bag," and no sooner were the words said than out jumped the stick, and beat the offenders soundly on the back till their clothes were in ribbons, and it did it all so quickly that the turn had come round to each of them before he was aware.

It was evening when the young turner reached the inn where his brothers had been so badly treated. He laid his bag down on the table, and began giving an account of all the wonderful things he had seen while going about the world.

"One may come across a wishing table," he said, "or an ass that gives gold, and such like; all very good things in their way, but not all of them put together are worth the treasure of which I have possession, and which I carry with me in that bag."

The landlord pricked up his ears. "What can it be?" he asked himself. "The bag must be filled with precious stones; I must try and get hold of that, cheaply too, for there is luck in odd numbers."

Bed-time came, and the guest stretched himself out on one of the benches and placed his bag under his head for a pillow. As soon as the landlord thought he was fast asleep, he went up to him and began gently and cautiously pulling and pushing at the bag to see if he could get it away and put another in its place.

But the young miller had been waiting for this, and just as the landlord was about to give a good last pull, he cried, "Cudgel, out of the bag," and the same moment the stick was out, and beginning its usual dance. It beat him with such a vengeance that the landlord cried out for mercy, but the louder his cries the more lustily did the stick beat time to them, until he fell to the ground exhausted.

"If you do not give up the wishing table and the gold ass," said the young turner, "the game shall begin over again."

"No, no," cried the landlord in a feeble voice, "I will give everything back, if only you will make that dreadful demon of a stick return to the bag."

"This time," said the turner, "I will deal with you according to mercy rather than justice, but beware of offending in like manner again." Then he cried, "Cudgel, into the bag," and let the man remain in peace.

The turner journeyed on next day to his father's house, taking with him the wishing table and the gold ass. The tailor was delighted to see his son again, and asked him, as he had the others, what trade he had learned since he left home.

"I am a turner, dear father," he answered.

"A highly skilled trade," said the tailor; "and what have you brought back with you from your travels?"

"An invaluable thing, dear father," replied the son; "a cudgel."

"What! a cudgel!" exclaimed the old man; "that was certainly well worth while, seeing that you can cut yourself one from the first tree you come across."

"But not such a one as this, dear father; for, if I say to it, 'Cudgel, out of the bag,' out it jumps, and gives any one who has evil intentions towards me such a bad time of it, that he falls down and cries for mercy. And know, that it was with this stick that I got back the wishing table and the gold ass, which the dishonest innkeeper stole from my brothers. Now, go and call them both here, and invite all your relations and friends, and I will feast them and fill their pockets with gold."

The old tailor was slow to believe all this, but nevertheless he went out and gathered his neighbours together. Then the turner put down a cloth, and led in the gold ass, and said to his brother, "Now, dear brother, speak to him." The miller said "Brickle-brit," and the cloth was immediately covered with gold pieces, which continued to pour from the ass's mouth until every one had taken as many as he could carry. (I see by your faces that you are all wishing you had been there.)

Then the turner brought in the wishing table, and said, "Now, dear brother, speak to it." And scarcely had the joiner cried, "Table, serve up a meal," than it was covered with a profusion of daintily dressed meats. Then the tailor and his guests sat down to a meal such as they had never enjoyed before in their lives, and they all sat up late into the night, full of good cheer and jollity.

The tailor put away his needle and thread, his yard-measure and his goose, and he and his three sons lived together henceforth in contentment and luxury.

Meanwhile, what had become of the goat, who had been the guilty cause of the three sons being driven from their home? I will tell you.

She was so ashamed of her shaven crown, that she ran and crept into a fox's hole. When the fox came home, he was met by two large glittering eyes that gleamed at him out of the darkness, and he was so frightened that he ran away. The bear met him, and perceiving that he was in some distress, said, "What is the matter, brother Fox? why are you pulling such a long face?" "Ah!" answered Red-skin, "there is a dreadful animal sitting in my hole, which glared at me with fiery eyes."

"We will soon drive him out," said the bear, and he trotted back with his friend to the hole and looked in, but the sight of the fiery eyes was quite enough for him, and he turned and took to his heels.

The bee met him, and noticing that he was somewhat ill at ease, said, "Bear, you look remarkably out of humour; where have you left your good spirits?" "It's easy for you to talk," replied the bear; "a horrible animal with red goggle-eyes is sitting in the fox's hole, and we cannot drive it out."

The bee said, "I really am sorry for you, Bear; I am but a poor weak little creature that you scarcely deign to look at in passing, but, for all that, I think I shall be able to help you."

With this the bee flew to the fox's hole, settled on the smooth shaven head of the goat, and stung her so violently, that she leaped high into the air, crying "Nan, nan!" and fled away like a mad thing into the open country; but no one, to this hour, has found out what became of her after that.

RUMPEL-STILTS-KEN,
OR
THE GOLD-SPINNER

By the side of a wood, in a country a long way off, ran a fine stream of water; and upon the stream there stood a mill. The miller's house was close by, and the miller, you must know, had a very beautiful daughter. She was, moreover, very shrewd and clever; and the miller was so proud of her, that he one day told the king of the land, who used to come and hunt in the wood, that his daughter could spin gold out of straw. Now this king was very fond of money; and when he heard the miller's boast his greediness was raised, and he sent for the girl to be brought before him. Then he led her to a chamber in his palace where there was a great heap of straw, and gave her a spinning-wheel, and said, "All this must be spun into gold before morning, as you love your life." It was in vain that the poor maiden said that it was only a silly boast of her father, for that she could do no such thing as spin straw into gold: the chamber door was locked, and she was left alone.

She sat down in one corner of the room, and began to bewail her hard fate; when on a sudden the door opened, and a droll-looking little man hobbled in, and said, "Good morrow to you, my good lass; what are you weeping for?" "Alas!" said she, "I must spin this straw into gold, and I know not how." "What will you give me," said the hobgoblin, "to do it for you?" "My necklace," replied the maiden. He took her at her word, and sat himself down to the wheel, and whistled and sang:

> *"Round about, round about,*
> *Lo and behold !*
> *Reel away, reel away,*
> *Straw into gold !"*

And round about the wheel went merrily; the work was quickly done, and the straw was all spun into gold.

When the king came and saw this, he was greatly astonished and pleased; but his heart grew still more greedy of gain, and he shut up the poor miller's daughter again with a fresh task. Then she knew not what to do, and sat down once more to weep; but the dwarf soon opened the door, and said, "What will you give me to do your task?" "The ring on my finger," said she. So her little friend took the ring, and began to work at the wheel again, and whistled and sang:

> *"Round about, round about,*
> *Lo and behold !*
> *Reel away, reel away,*
> *Straw into gold !"*

till, long before morning, all was done again.

The king was greatly delighted to see all this glittering treasure; but still he had not enough: so he took the miller's daughter to a yet larger heap, and said, "All this must be spun to-night; and if it is, you shall be my queen." As soon as she was alone the dwarf came in, and said, "What will you give me to spin gold for you this third time?" "I have nothing left," said she. "Then say you will give me," said the little man, "the first little child that you may have when you are queen." "That may never be," thought the miller's daughter: and as she knew no other way to get her task done, she said she would do what he asked. Round went the wheel again to the old song, and the manikin once more spun the heap into gold. The king came in the morning, and, finding all he wanted, was forced to keep his word; so he married the miller's daughter, and she really became queen.

At the birth of her first little child she was very glad, and forgot the dwarf, and what she had said. But one day he came into her room, where she was sitting playing with her baby, and put her in mind of it. Then she grieved sorely at her misfortune, and said she would give him all the wealth of the kingdom if he would let her off, but in vain; till at last her tears softened him, and he said, "I will give you three days' grace, and if during that time you tell me my name, you shall keep your child."

Now the queen lay awake all night, thinking of all the odd names that she had ever heard; and she sent messengers all over the land to find out new ones. The next day the little man came, and she began with TIMOTHY, ICHABOD, BENJAMIN, JEREMIAH, and all the names she could remember; but to all and each of them he said, "Madam, that is not my name."

The second day she began with all the comical names she could hear of, BANDY-LEGS, HUNCH-BACK, CROOK-SHANKS, and so on; but the little gentleman still said to every one of them, "Madam, that is not my name."

The third day one of the messengers came back, and said, "I travelled two days without hearing of any other names; but yesterday, as I was climbing a high hill, among the trees of the forest where the fox and the hare bid each other good night, I saw a little hut; and before the hut burnt a fire; and round about the fire a funny little dwarf was dancing upon one leg, and singing:

> *"'Merrily the feast I'll make.*
> *To-day I'll brew, to-morrow bake;*
> *Merrily I'll dance and sing,*
> *For next day will a stranger bring.*
> *Little does my lady dream*
> *Rumpel-stilts-ken is my name!'"*

When the queen heard this she jumped for joy, and as soon as her little friend came she sat down upon her throne, and called all her court round to enjoy the fun; and the nurse stood by her side with the baby in her arms, as if it was quite ready to be given up. Then the little man began to chuckle at the thoughts of having the poor child to take home with him to his hut in the woods; and he cried out, "Now, lady, what is my name?" "Is it JOHN?" asked she. "No, madam!" "Is it TOM?" "No, madam!" "Is it JEMMY?" "It is not." "Can your name be RUMPEL-STILTS-KEN?" said the lady slily.

"Some witch told you that!—some witch told you that!" cried the little man, and dashed his right foot in a rage so deep into the floor, that he was forced to lay hold of it with both hands to pull it out.

Then he made the best of his way off, while the nurse laughed and the baby crowed; and all the court jeered at him for having had so much trouble for nothing, and said, "We wish you a very good morning, and a merry feast, Mr. RUMPEL-STILTS-KEN!"

GIANT GOLDEN-BEARD

In a country village, over the hills and far away, lived a poor man, who had an only son born to him. Now this child was born under a lucky star, and was therefore what the people of that country call a Luck's-child; and those who told his fortune said, that in his fourteenth year he would marry no less a lady than the king's own daughter.

It so happened that the king of that land, soon after the child's birth, passed through the village in disguise, and stopping at the blacksmith's shop, asked what news was stirring. "Good news!" said the people. "Master Brock, down that lane, has just had a child born to him that they say is a Luck's-child; and we are told that, when he is fourteen years old, he is fated to marry our noble king's daughter." This did not please the king; so he went to the poor child's parents, and asked them whether they would sell him their son. "No," said they. But the stranger begged very hard, and said he would give a great deal of money: so as they had scarcely bread to eat, they at last agreed, saying to themselves, "He is a Luck's-child; all, therefore, is no doubt for the best —he can come to no harm."

The king took the child, put it into a box, and rode away; but when he came to a deep stream he threw it into the current, and said to himself, "That young gentleman will never be my daughter's husband." The box, however, floated down the stream. Some kind fairy watched over it, so that no water reached the child; and at last, about two miles from the king's chief city, it stopped at the dam of a mill. The miller soon saw it, and took a long pole and drew it towards the shore, and finding it heavy, thought there was gold inside; but when he opened it he found a pretty little boy that smiled upon him merrily. Now the miller and his wife had no children, and they therefore rejoiced to see their prize, saying, "Heaven has sent it to us"; so they treated it very kindly, and brought it up with such care that every one liked and loved it.

About thirteen years passed over their heads, when the same king came by chance to the mill, and seeing the boy, asked the miller if that was his son. "No," said he, "I found him, when a babe, floating down the river in a box into the mill-dam." "How long ago?" asked the king. "Some thirteen years," said the miller. "He is a fine fellow," said the king; "can you spare him to carry a letter to the queen? It will please me very much, and I will give him two pieces of gold for his trouble." "As your majesty pleases," said the miller.

Now the king had guessed at once that this must be the child he had tried to drown, so he wrote a letter by him to the queen, saying, "As soon as the bearer of this reaches you, let him be killed and buried, so that all may be over before I come back."

The young man set out with this letter but missed his way, and came in the evening to a dark wood. Through the gloom he saw a light afar off, to which he bent his steps, and found that it came from a little cottage. There was no one within except an old woman, who was frightened at seeing him, and said, "Why do you come hither, and whither are you going?" "I am going to the queen, to whom I was to have given a letter; but I have lost my way, and shall be glad if you will give me a night's rest." "You are very unlucky," said she, "for this is a robbers' hut; and if the band come back while you are here it may be worse for you." "I am so tired, however," replied he, "that I must take my chance, for I can go no further"; so he laid the letter on the table, stretched himself out upon a bench, and fell asleep.

When the robbers came home and saw him, they asked the old woman who the strange lad was. "I have given him shelter for charity," said she; "he had a letter to carry to the queen, and lost his way." The robbers took up the letter, broke it open, and read the orders which were in it to murder the bearer. Then their leader was very angry at the king's trick; so he tore his letter, and wrote a fresh one, begging the queen, as soon as the young man reached her, to marry him to the princess. Meantime they let him sleep on till morning broke, and then showed him the right way to the queen's palace; where, as soon as she had read the letter, she made all ready for the wedding: and as the young man was very handsome, the princess was very dutiful, and took him then and there for a husband.

After a while the king came back; and when he saw that this Luck's-child was married to the princess, notwithstanding all the art and cunning he had used to thwart his luck, he asked eagerly how all this had happened, and what were the orders which he had given. "Dear husband," said the queen, "here is your own letter—read it for yourself." The king took it, and seeing that an exchange had been made, asked his son-in-law what he had done with the letter he gave him to carry. "I know nothing of it," said he; "if it is not the one you gave me, it must have been taken away in the night when I slept." Then the king was very wroth and said, "No man shall have my daughter who does not go down into the wonderful cave and bring me three golden hairs from the beard of the giant king who reigns there; do this, and you shall have my free leave to be my daughter's husband." "I will soon do that," said the youth; so he took leave of his wife and set out on his journey.

At the first city that he came to, the guard at the gate stopped him, and asked what trade he followed, and what he knew. "I know everything," said he. "If that be so," said they, "you are just the man we want; be so good as to find out why our fountain in the market-place is dry, and will give no water. Tell us the cause of that, and we will give you two asses loaded with gold." "With all my heart," said he, "when I come back."

Then he journeyed on, and came to another city, and there the guard also asked him what trade he followed, and what he understood. "I know everything," answered he. "Then pray do us a good turn," said they; "tell us why a tree, which always before bore us golden apples, does not even bear a leaf this year." "Most willingly," said he, "as I come back."

At last his way led him to the side of a great lake of water, over which he must pass. The ferryman soon began to ask, as the others had done, what was his trade, and what he knew. "Everything," said he. "Then," said the other, "pray tell me why I am forced for ever to ferry over this water, and have never been able to get my freedom; I will reward you handsomely." "Ferry me over," said the young man, "and I will tell you all about it as I come home."

When he had passed the water, he came to the wonderful cave. It looked very black and gloomy; but the wizard king was not at home, and his grandmother sat at the door in her easy-chair. "What do you want?" said she. "Three golden hairs from the giant's beard," answered he. "You will run a great risk," said she, "when he comes home; yet I will try what I can do for you." Then she changed him into an ant, and told him to hide himself in the folds of her cloak. "Very well," said he: "but I want also to know why the city fountain is dry; why the tree that bore golden apples is now leafless; and what it is that binds the ferryman to his post." "You seem fond of asking puzzling things," said the old dame; "but

lie still, and listen to what the giant says when I pull
the golden hairs, and perhaps you may learn what
you want." Soon night set in, and the old gentleman
came home. As soon as he entered he began to snuff
up the air, and cried, "All is not right here: I smell
man's flesh." Then he searched all round in vain,
and the old dame scolded, and said, "Why should
you turn everything topsy-turvy? I have just set all
straight." Upon this he laid his head in her lap, and
soon fell asleep. As soon as he began to snore, she
seized one of the golden hairs of his beard and pulled
it out. "Mercy!" cried he, starting up: "what are
you about?" "I had a dream that roused me," said
she, "and in my trouble I seized hold of your hair.
I dreamt that the fountain in the market-place of
the city was become dry, and would give no water;
what can be the cause?" "Ah! if they could find that
out they would be glad," said the giant: "under a
stone in the fountain sits a toad; when they kill him,
it will flow again."

This said, he fell asleep, and the old lady pulled out
another hair. "What would you be at?" cried he in
a rage. "Don't be angry," said she, "I did it in my
sleep; I dreamt that I was in a great kingdom a long
way off, and that there was a beautiful tree there,
that used to bear golden apples, but that now has
not even a leaf upon it; what is the meaning of that?"
"Aha!" said the giant, "they would like very well
to know that. At the root of the tree a mouse is
gnawing; if they were to kill him, the tree would

bear golden apples again: if not, it will soon die. Now do let me sleep in peace; if you wake me again, you shall rue it."

Then he fell once more asleep; and when she heard him snore she pulled out the third golden hair, and the giant jumped up and threatened her sorely; but she soothed him, and said, "It was a very strange dream I had this time: methought I saw a ferryman, who was bound to ply backwards and forwards over a great lake, and could never find out how to set himself free; what is the charm that binds him?" "A silly fool!" said the giant: "if he were to give the rudder into the hand of any passenger that came, he would find himself free, and the other would be forced to take his place. Now pray let me sleep."

In the morning the giant arose and went out; and the old woman gave the young man the three golden hairs, reminded him of the three answers, and sent him on his way.

He soon came to the ferryman, who knew him again, and asked for the answer which he had said he would give him. "Ferry me over first," said he, "and then I will tell you." When the boat reached the other side, he told him to give the rudder to the first passenger that came, and then he might run away as soon as he pleased. The next place that he came to was the city where the barren tree stood: "Kill the mouse," said he, "that is gnawing the tree's root, and you will have golden apples again." They gave him a rich gift for this news, and he journeyed on to the city where the fountain had dried up; and the guard asked him how to make the water flow. So he told them how to cure that mischief, and they thanked him, and gave him the two asses laden with gold.

And now at last this Luck's-child reached home, and his wife was very glad to see him, and to hear how well everything had gone with him. Then he gave the three golden hairs to the king, who could no longer deny him, though he was at heart quite as spiteful against his son-in-law as ever. The gold, however, astonished him, and when he saw all the treasure he cried out with joy, "My dear son, where did you find all this gold?" "By the side of a lake," said the youth, "where there is plenty more to be had." "Pray tell me where it lies," said the king, "that I may go and get some too." "As much as you please," replied the other. "You must set out and travel on and on, till you come to the shore of a great lake: there you will see a ferryman; let him carry you across, and when once you are over, you will see gold as plentiful as sand upon the shore."

Away went the greedy king; and when he came to the lake he beckoned to the ferryman, who gladly took him into his boat; and as soon as he was there gave the rudder into his hand and sprang ashore, leaving the old king to ferry away, as a reward for his craftiness and treachery.

"And is his majesty plying there to this day?" You may be sure of that, for nobody will trouble himself to take the rudder out of his hands.

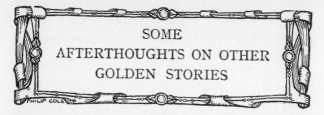

SOME
AFTERTHOUGHTS ON OTHER
GOLDEN STORIES

THE story told by John Ruskin was written, as we have seen, "all out of his own head." But the Golden Stories you have just read were not invented by anyone. If you have read a story called *Uncle Tom's Cabin*, you will know that when someone asked a little black girl named Topsy who made her, she answered, "I dunno; specks I growed." It is the same with these stories—I specks they growed. They have been told again and again for hundreds of years in country places on the Continent and in England, handed down from grandmother to grandchildren by word of mouth, and sometimes a little altered in the telling, but always the same in a general way. Such stories as these are called folk-tales, because they have been told among the folk or ordinary people from generation to generation.

Now let us think over each story in turn as we did with *The King of the Golden River*.

THE GOLDEN GOOSE

Three sons again, and the reader's special attention and sympathy asked at once for the youngest. Ruskin *did* borrow something from the folk-tales after all!

Gluck and Dummling! Think of *The King of the Golden River* as you read on.

Is there any laugh in Ruskin's story? There is not only a laugh in this story but an idea as well—that if a person steals a thing he finds it difficult to get rid of it; but I do not think the first people who told this story troubled about any moral.

Compare the gold of Ruskin's tale with the gold of the goose story.

Do you think that a good school play could be made from this story?

What is the surprise in this story? What did you expect when the three girls came into the tale?

THE WISHING TABLE, ETC.

Three sons again, you see.

Where is the first pause in the story? The second? And so on.

Would the young man with the table be welcomed at the wayside inns? What mistake did the joiner make?

Who is the central villain in this story?

Who is the hero?

The tale is full of good pictures. Which picture do you consider the most striking?

Would this story make a good play? Has it any moral?

What place does gold take in it? Which sentence shows that at first it was told rather than written? What part do girls or women play in the tale?

Rumpel-stilts-ken, or the Gold-Spinner

There are no three sons in this story, nor three daughters; but the number three does come into it. How?

How did the king *propose* to the miller's daughter?

The old story-tellers did not trouble much about fairness or justice. Did the king deserve all he got? Or the queen?

What do you consider the best picture in the story?

Giant Golden-Beard

One son only in this story!

One of our poets has a story called "The Man born to be King." There is a king with a child in a box, as well as a miller, in this tale also.[1] Do you think this title would suit the present story?

What is the *idea* which runs through this tale?

What place does gold take in this story?

Was it really luck which made this young man succeed? If not, what was it?

[1] See *Atalanta's Race and Other Stories* by William Morris ("Kings' Treasuries," No. 84).

SELECTION OF TITLES

GRADED AND ARRANGED UNDER SUBJECTS

The ages mentioned in this list are only approximate; in choosing the books teachers should make allowance for local conditions and the ability of the pupils.

KINGS TREASURIES OF LITERATURE

ALLEGORY, MYTHOLOGY, FAIRY TALES, etc.

For Junior Forms (Ages 10–13)

10. THE ADVENTURES OF ODYSSEUS. Retold from Homer in English prose by F. S. Marvin, R. J. G. Mayor, and F. M. Stawell. 224 pp.

With a simple Introduction, a complete Pronouncing Index of Proper Names, and an Epilogue dealing with the stories told about Homer and Homeric poetry. The Illustrations help greatly in re-creating the environment of the *Odyssey*, from which the tale of the wanderings is directly drawn.

14. A WONDER-BOOK FOR BOYS AND GIRLS. By NATHANIEL HAWTHORNE. Edited by E. M. Wilmot Buxton. 256 pp.

This book contains the stories of The Gorgon's Head; The Golden Touch; The Paradise of Children; The Three Golden Apples; The Miraculous Pitcher; and the Chimæra. With simple explanatory footnotes, a Commentary containing Exercises, an Essay on hero-stories, and a Pronouncing Index of Proper Names.

24. THE HEROES. By CHARLES KINGSLEY. Edited by E. M. Wilmot Buxton. 224 pp.

Footnotes are provided as well as a useful Commentary containing a Life of Kingsley, Exercises, and a Pronouncing Index of Proper Names.

38. THE PILGRIM'S PROGRESS. Slightly abridged from Part I of the Allegory by JOHN BUNYAN. Edited by the late Margaret A. Gilliland, M.A., with a dramatized version by N. T. Carrington, M.A. Illustrated. 256 pp.

This edition has been specially prepared for those teachers who hesitate to use Bunyan's great work because of its theology, and who yet wish to introduce their pupils to the great Allegory as a story of adventure.

50. STORIES FROM LE MORTE D'ARTHUR and the Mabinogion. By BEATRICE CLAY. 192 pp.

This book contains the full story of Arthur and the Round Table told simply after the style of the originals.

60. THE WATER BABIES. By CHARLES KINGSLEY. Abridged and Edited by Lucy Menzies. 224 pp.

The abridgment has been skilfully made so as to leave the story complete in itself. A life of the author, suitable for younger children's reading, appears at the end of the volume.

94 THE CANTERBURY PILGRIMS. By MARY STURT, M.A., and ELLEN C. OAKDEN, M.A. Illustrated. 160 pp.

In simple language the authors have attempted to give younger pupils not merely a collection of 'Stories from Chaucer,' but a complete idea of the *Canterbury Tales*, and the people who told them, together with the interesting circumstances of their immortal journey.

119. THE KING OF THE GOLDEN RIVER. By JOHN RUSKIN. *To which are added for comparison*, THE BLACK BROTHERS, AND OTHER STORIES. 128 pp.

Containing full text of Ruskin's story, with the original Doyle illustrations.

141. THE ROSE AND THE RING. By W. M. THACKERAY.
Edited by Phyllis M. Preston. 192 pp.
Thackeray's famous fairy-tale with his original pictures.

170. TANGLEWOOD TALES. By NATHANIEL HAWTHORNE.
Edited by Guy N. Pocock, M.A. Illustrated by W. H.
Birch. 256 pp.

186. NORSE LEGENDS. Retold from the Eddas by MRS
STEPHEN HOBHOUSE. 256 pp.
These are delightful legends of the Norse gods and goddesses retold by
an author who is well known as a lecturer on the art of telling stories
for children. These stories of the gods and goddesses, giants and
dwarfs, and strange beasts of Norse mythology are more than mere
tales retold, for the author has gone back to the Eddas, and so has been
able to keep the strong, rugged, yet strangely childlike spirit of the
originals, and also their very close bearing on natural phenomena.
The book is equally suitable for junior and older pupils.

195. ALICE IN WONDERLAND, with The Hunting of the
Snark, and Poems from *Sylvie and Bruno*. By LEWIS
CARROLL, with the original illustrations by the author.
192 pp.

**198. ROBIN HOOD AND OTHER TALES OF OLD
ENGLAND.** Retold by MRS STEPHEN HOBHOUSE.
Illustrated. 256 pp.
Admirable as old ballads are, there are a great many children, and
teachers too, who prefer the stories in prose. Mrs Hobhouse, the
author of *Norse Legends* in this series, has retold the most famous of
the Robin Hood stories, and other old English tales, in her own
inimitable style. Suggestions for composition included.

241. STORIES FROM DANTE. By E. BIGG-WITHER. 192 pp.
Dante's masterpiece, *The Divine Comedy*, is here told in quite simple
language, and the author, a distinguished Italian scholar, has cleverly
contrived to keep the spirit of the original.

For Lower Middle Forms (Ages 12–14)

21. TALES FROM ANDERSEN. Edited and selected by Reed
   Moorhouse. 256 pp.

37. THE STORY OF THE 'ILIAD.' Retold from Homer
   by F. S. MARVIN, R. J. G. MAYOR, and F. M. STAWELL.
   With Portrait of Achilles. 224 pp.
This volume is uniform with *The Adventures of Odysseus* (*See* No. 10).

87. RIP VAN WINKLE and Other Stories. By WASHINGTON
   IRVING. 192 pp.
In addition to the title-story this volume contains The Legend of Sleepy
Hollow, Westminster Abbey, and The Sketch Book.

231. CELTIC LEGENDS. By MICHAEL O'GRADY, B.A., and
   J. B. NELSON, B.A. 256 pp.
A valuable and readable collection. Test questions included.

THE BIBLE AS LITERATURE

85. A BIBLE ANTHOLOGY. 256 pp.
The compiler has collected in this little volume a number of passages
from the Old and New Testaments (Authorized Version) which can be
used in the ordinary English lesson as examples of the many and varied
literary forms which are included in Hebrew literature and in the
English renderings of New Testament Greek.

BIOGRAPHY

232. SEVENTY YEARS A SHOWMAN. By 'LORD' GEORGE
SANGER. With an Introduction by Kenneth Grahame.
216 pp.

This book, the autobiography of a world-famous showman, is a vivid
picture of England as Charles Dickens must have seen it. The essay
which is printed as an introduction to the book is considered by some
to be, as literature, Kenneth Grahame's finest work.

DRAMA

For ages 12–14

12. FORM-ROOM PLAYS—JUNIOR BOOK—FIRST SERIES.
Compiled from Literature by Evelyn Smith, B.A. 256 pp.

Containing the following pieces dramatized from the original sources,
with full stage and costume directions: The Swineherd (Hans Andersen);
The Parlement of Foules (Chaucer); Thor's Hammer (Norse Folklore);
The Death of Balder (Norse Folklore): The Travelling Companion
(Hans Andersen); The Cock and the Fox (Chaucer); A Christmas
Carol (Charles Dickens); The Perfect Holiday (L. M. Alcott's *Little
Women*); Alice in Wonderland (Lewis Carroll); Circe's Palace (Haw-
thorne's *Tanglewood Tales*); Robin Hood (Old English Ballad); The
Lady of the Lake (Sir Walter Scott); A Midsummer Night's Dream
(William Shakespeare).

110. THE BEAU OF BATH AND FIVE OTHER ONE-ACT PLAYS.
By CONSTANCE D'ARCY MACKAY. 128 pp.

These six plays are not only beautifully written by a well-known
American dramatist, but they serve to introduce some of the most
interesting figures of the period of Beau Nash, Burke, and Fanny
Burney. Each play is short enough for school acting and very few
accessories are required.

5

131. FORM-ROOM PLAYS—INTERMEDIATE BOOK.
Compiled by Evelyn Smith, B.A. 224 pp.

Containing the following pieces dramatized with full stage and costume directions: The Goosegirl (Grimm); The Town Mouse and the Country Mouse; The Shepherdess and the Chimney Sweeper (Andersen); A Visit to London; The Fool of Dunvegan; Havelok the Dane; The Enchantment of Finn; Gudrun (Germanic legend); The Siege of Ping (Chinese legend); The Kitchen Knight (Malory); The Marchioness (Dickens); The Escape from Lochleven (Scott); Alice and the Caterpillar.

184. PLAYS FOR MIDDLE FORMS. Edited by Reed
Moorhouse. 256 pp.

A collection of delightful plays particularly suitable for middle forms, including Brother Sun (Laurence Housman); The Only Legend, a Masque of the Scarlet Pierrot (John Drinkwater); The Ox and the Ass (Hilary Pepler); An Old Wives' Tale, adapted (George Peele); Goblin Market, adapted and dramatized (Christina Rossetti); Piper's Pool (Helen H. A. Hope); Six who pass while the Lentils Boil (Stuart Walker); The Life and Death of Tom Thumb the Great, adapted (Henry Fielding); Everyman (adapted); Selling his Ancestors from *The School for Scandal.*

206. CLASS-ROOM PLAYS FROM GREAT NOVELS.
Adapted by Dora Hollom, B.A. 192 pp.

Experience has proved that the dialogue portions of famous novels put into dramatic form make admirable reading in class. Miss Dora Hollom, the well-known author and teacher, has made a selection of scenes from the great novels, including *Westward Ho!*, *Cranford*, *The Last Days of Pompeii*, and *A Tale of Two Cities*, and has arranged them as class-room plays.

220. FORM-ROOM PLAYS FOR GIRLS. By E. R. and
L. W. FARADAY. 224 pp.

Thirteen plays, charming in themselves and based on delightful stories, suitable for girls. Hints on the plays and the airs of the songs are provided. The plays included are The Plaining Song; The Potion of Lao-Tsze; The Discreet Kadiga; The Three Spinners; The Treasure of the Alhambra; Dominion; Cosmo, the Woodcutter; The Countess's Pearls; The Best Wish; Morozko; The Child in the Snow; Princess Félise; Thorwald's Bridal.

252. JUNIOR FORM-ROOM PLAYS—Second Series. By Dorothy and Diana Scott. 192 pp.

Containing the following little plays adapted from well-known stories: Ameliaranne; Tom Sawyer; Through the Looking-glass; Rip Van Winkle; The Rose and the Ring; David Copperfield with his Aunt; The Pied Piper; The Tinder-box; Hansel and Gretel; The Pilgrim's Progress; The Pardoner's Tale; King John and the Abbot of Canterbury; Get up and bar the Door; Joseph and his Brethren; David and Goliath.

For ages 14 and over

65. FORM-ROOM PLAYS—SENIOR BOOK. Compiled from English Literature by Evelyn Smith, B.A. 256 pp., including 10 pp. of Music.

Containing dramatized pieces from *The Mill on the Floss, Quentin Durward, Nicholas Nickleby, The Vicar of Wakefield, Northanger Abbey,* and *Comus,* as well as specially prepared passages from Sheridan's *The Critic* and Ben Jonson's *The Alchemist.*

126. THE RIVALS. By Richard Brinsley Sheridan. Edited by John Hampden, M.A. 192 pp.

This favourite classic is given in full, but it has been specially arranged for acting in school. Unsuitable parts are enclosed in brackets.

147. THE SHOEMAKER'S HOLIDAY. By Thomas Dekker. Edited by Guy N. Pocock, M.A. 160 pp.

A school edition—not an abridgment—of this delightful citizen play, with a full Commentary containing Questions and Exercises, also an Acting Appendix.

149. SHE STOOPS TO CONQUER. By Oliver Goldsmith. Edited by John Hampden, M.A. 192 pp.

With a Commentary containing Questions and Exercises and an Acting Appendix.

ALPHABETICAL LIST OF TITLES

8

Kings Treasuries

Kings Treasuries

Kings Treasuries

Kings Treasuries